M000307606

WHIPCRACK!

The banker had extended his arm for a final hand-shake, and Longarm was putting out his own hand, when a rifle's unmistakeable high-pitched bark broke the stillness of the deserted street. The rifle slug whistled between the two men, and the air created by the speeding bullet brushed Longarm's face as the lead chunk thudded into the wall of the bank behind them.

Longarm dropped safely to the ground. But another shot cracked and the banker's body buckled as the rifle slug tore into him and knocked him back against the door frame. He slid slowly down the frame of the door and sprawled lifeless on the ground.

Drawing his revolver, Longarm tried to locate the source of the shots. Before he could get a fix on the sniper, another shot barked. . . .

*   *   *

SPECIAL PREVIEW!

Turn to the back of this book for a special excerpt from an exciting new western . . .

Gunpoint

. . . The shattering story of a deadly blood feud by America's new star of the classic western, Giles Tippette.

DON'T MISS THESE
ALL-ACTION WESTERN SERIES
FROM THE BERKLEY PUBLISHING GROUP

THE GUNSMITH by J. R. Roberts
 Clint Adams was a legend among lawmen, outlaws, and ladies. They called him . . . the Gunsmith.

LONGARM by Tabor Evans
 The popular long-running series about U.S. Deputy Marshal Long—his life, his loves, his fight for justice.

LONE STAR by Wesley Ellis
 The blazing adventures of Jessica Starbuck and the martial arts master, Ki. Over eight million copies in print.

SLOCUM by Jake Logan
 Today's longest-running action western. John Slocum rides a deadly trail of hot blood and cold steel.

TABOR EVANS

LONGARM

AND THE DOUBLE EAGLES

JOVE BOOKS, NEW YORK

If you purchased this book without a cover you should be aware that this book is stolen property. It was reported as "unsold and destroyed" to the publisher and neither the author nor the publisher has received any payment for this "stripped book."

LONGARM AND THE DOUBLE EAGLES

A Jove Book / published by arrangement with
the author

PRINTING HISTORY
Jove edition / October 1992

All rights reserved.
Copyright © 1992 by Jove Publications, Inc.
Gunpoint excerpt copyright © 1992 by Giles Tippette.
This book may not be reproduced in whole
or in part, by mimeograph or any other means,
without permission. For information address:
The Berkley Publishing Group,
200 Madison Avenue,
New York, New York 10016.

ISBN: 0-515-10955-X

Jove Books are published by The Berkley Publishing Group,
200 Madison Avenue, New York, New York 10016.
The name "JOVE" and the "J" logo
are trademarks belonging to Jove Publications, Inc.

PRINTED IN THE UNITED STATES OF AMERICA

10 9 8 7 6 5 4 3 2

LONGARM

AND THE DOUBLE EAGLES

Chapter 1

Longarm had been leaning on the bar before the shooting started. He was holding his empty shotglass in one hand, listening to the raucous tinkling of the battered honky-tonk piano that stood against the side wall of the half-empty saloon. When the jingling ended, the pianist who'd been fingering the keyboard swept his thumb across the keys, then lifted both hands high with his fingers outspread to signal that he'd be taking a rest for a little while.

Longarm called to the piano-player. "Come on over here, friend. I'll be right pleased to stand you a drink, because you been playing some mighty fine music."

When the musician was within a step of reaching him, Longarm gestured to summon the barkeep. Somehow the thick shotglass slipped from his hand and dropped to land with a muffled thud on the sawdust-covered floor.

Longarm bent down to pick up the glass, and as he stretched out his arm to close his hand on it, bending still further, a shot cracked from the swinging doors. The slug from the pistol of the invisible gun-wielder whistled through the air above Longarm's head. It flew past him and hit the back bar's mirrored wall with a crash of splintering glass.

Longarm did not stand up, but relaxed and let himself fall flat on the floor. He swept his Colt out of its holster as he dropped and triggered off two quick rounds, snap-shooting toward the swinging doors. His first bullet grazed the frame of one of the batwings, flapping it open again to the accompanying noise of splintering wood. His next shot whistled out through the small empty space between the batwings.

A loud yell sounded from outside the door even before the echoes of the shot had died away inside the saloon. Expecting a shot in reply to his, Longarm held his fire and did not move from his sprawled-out position on the floor. When he heard boot heels thunking across the narrow porch of the saloon's front he levered himself to his feet.

This time he slanted his course away from the center of the saloon as he started running toward the doorway. He ignored the loud shouts from the small handful of men widely spaced along the bar. As he ran, Longarm fixed his attention on the open space that gaped between the bottom of the doors and the floor, but he saw no booted feet on the narrow porch.

Only four stretching steps were needed to take Longarm to the doorway. As he neared the batwings he extended both arms to push the doors wide apart. Through the first tiny crack as they opened he caught a glimpse of a man running down the middle of the street, away from the saloon.

"You there!" Longarm shouted, pushing away the door that was pressing on his gun hand and preventing him from shooting with his usual accuracy. "Stop right now or I'll shoot!"

Longarm was not surprised when his command was not obeyed; he knew that a lead bullet spoke with an authority no voice could match. The retreating gunman was not

2

looking back. He was hunched forward, his head lowered, keeping his legs churning as he fled down the narrow street.

Longarm turned sideways to free his gun hand from the door's pressure, and when he turned back he saw the fleeing man had vanished from sight. His disappearance was so unexpected that Longarm froze, scanning the deserted street, trying to pick out where he'd last caught sight of his quarry.

Longarm saw nothing until he began running down the street. Then he spotted the little gap that yawned between two of the weather-beaten store buildings that lined both sides of the narrow dirt street, and headed toward it. Though there was still a faint line of sunset-pink glowing above the bit of horizon visible at the end of the street, when Longarm reached the narrow opening between the two buildings it was darkened to a gloomy shadow.

Peering into·the open space in the fast-waning daylight revealed nothing. Longarm took a half step ahead, but just as he was turning his eyes away he caught a glimpse of motion. Before he could blink, a hand holding a pistol appeared, outlined darkly against the narrow rectangle of clear sky visible at the end of the open space between the buildings.

Longarm was ready when the muzzle of the revolver moved a bit, a sign that the unseen man holding it was preparing to take aim but, though he still had a finger tensed on the trigger of his Colt, Longarm still did not trigger off a shot. He waited, hoping his unknown assailant would offer him a better target.

Almost at once Longarm's patience was rewarded. He glimpsed the partial silhouette of the man who'd run from him as the retreating gunman edged into the narrow opening again.

Longarm called, "Stop where you're at and drop that gun! I got you cold in my sights and if you even look like you're going to try for a shot, you'll be dead before you can trigger it!"

As clear and positive as Longarm's warning had been, the man he'd cautioned chose to ignore it. Longarm saw the muzzle of the threatening revolver shift once more; then the fugitive's torso came into full view as he swiveled, looking for a better angle of aim. Longarm dropped to one knee, raising his Colt as he moved. His shot echoed that of his unknown assailant so quickly that the two shots blended into what sounded like a single unusually loud report.

Longarm heard the other man's bullet scrape its course along the wall of one of the buildings that formed the narrow gap. His own slug flew true. It struck the man who'd fired first, knocking him to the ground.

Still cautious in spite of his certainty that he'd loosed a killing shot, Longarm began scrabbling through the narrow gap on all fours. He twisted his broad shoulders from side to side in the constricted space to keep from getting caught up as he moved. His Colt was still grasped in his right hand, his eyes fixed on the head and shoulders of the prone and motionless form of his still-unknown adversary.

Before he'd reached the body at the end of the passageway, one of the men who'd been in the saloon looked through the gap between the buildings, and called to the others who'd run out of the saloon after Longarm.

"They're over here!" the man called.

Twisting to shift in the narrow space, Longarm shouted over his shoulder. "We got a dead man here. And it's got dark so fast that we'll have to carry him over to the saloon before we can take a good look at him."

By this time the other men who'd been in the saloon were crowding into the slit between the buildings. Longarm decided to go on to the end of the building instead of trying to push his way out. He reached the end of the narrow space and stepped over the recumbent body of the man who'd been trying to kill him. The fading light that had been dim only moments earlier had now given way to darkness.

Sliding his Colt back into its holster, Longarm fingered a match from his vest pocket and flicked its head with his iron-hard thumbnail. He brought the burning match as close as possible to the dead man's face and found it vaguely familiar. But even when he held the flickering match close to the body he could not put a name to the dead man.

Stepping across the body, Longarm waited while the other men who'd been in the saloon pushed their way into the open space behind the row of buildings. An outburst of voices greeted him, such a loud babble that it seemed as though every man in the crowd was talking at once.

Raising his voice again, Longarm commanded, "Some of you men pick this fellow up and carry him back to the saloon. And you better look around and see if you can find his gun. It must have got knocked out of his hand when I shot him. Whoever finds it, I'd be obliged if he'd bring it to me. I'll be at the saloon and I want to have a look at it later on."

Somehow the half-dozen men who'd followed Longarm managed to carry out his instructions, though the four who'd picked up the shooter's corpse were forced to carry it along the backs of the buildings until they encountered a space between the structures that was wide enough to accommodate them and their load. They were starting up the saloon's steps when the barkeep pushed through the batwings and saw them.

"Now, what in hell do you fellows think you're doing?" he asked, his voice almost raised to a shout. "My place ain't no funeral parlor! Either dump that dead man out here on the street, or lug him down the street to Swenson's Furniture Store! Take it right on through to the back room; that's where they keep the coffins."

"Just hold on a minute, friend," Longarm said, keeping his voice as low as possible while still trying to be heard over the increasingly loud and excited chatter of the group that had carried the body. "These fellows are all going to want a drink, and they sure ain't going to get none at a furniture store."

"That don't make no difference," the barkeep said.

Longarm stepped closer to the barkeep and lowered his voice. "Even if these fellows here wasn't a likely bunch of customers, I'd still tell 'em to carry this dead man right on in to your place. I want to look at him where there's light enough to see, and far as I can see I figure your place has got the best light close by. Now, I'd sure hate to have to use my badge to get you to change your mind, but if that's how you—"

"All right, Marshal Long," the barkeep said hurriedly. "I know I was wrong. You fellows go on and carry that dead man inside so the marshal here can get a good look at his face. Then the drinks are on me for whoever helps lug that body down to the furniture store where it belongs."

Longarm waited outside the saloon while the crowd that had formed around the door went inside. Then he went inside himself and raised his voice to override the chatter of voices.

"Now, all of you shut up for a minute and listen to me!" he called. "My name's Long, Custis Long, and I'm a deputy United States marshal. I got a few questions I need to ask you men."

"Ask away," one of the men in the group said quickly. "Not that it's likely we know much to tell you. Me, I got a pretty good look at that dead man, but I sure don't recall that I ever set eyes on him before."

A chorus of voices rose quickly as the others in the group spoke up to deny ever having seen the dead man before. Longarm waited until the medley had died away.

"All right," he said. "Now I only got one question to start with. Did any of you men pick up that dead man's gun? Or anything else he might've dropped?"

A second murmur of voices swept over the dozen or more men who'd appeared when the shots fired by Longarm and his assailant had broken the quiet of the small cluster of buildings that was the core of the town. Longarm let them chatter for a moment, then went on.

"I can't promise you no reward," he said. "But I got a hankering to take a good look at that six-gun. Then, after I get back to my office in Denver, I can likely send a few dollars to whoever's got it now, if he hands it over to me right away. And don't try to put me off with no hogwash. I know one of you is bound to have that pistol, and whichever of you men it is, I'd sure hate to have to arrest you for trying to get away with evidence you stole."

A single voice broke the silence that had fallen on the group after Longarm had spoken. The voice came from a man near the center of the crowd. "I picked up his gun, Marshal. I sure didn't give no mind to it being evidence, but if you say it'll help you, why, you're welcome to it, no reward needed."

"Oh, his six-gun's gun's evidence, all right, so I'd reckon you better hand it over to me," Longarm replied. "And I'll see about the reward just the same. That gun might help me find out who the dead man is, if he ain't got anything else on him that'll give me a lead."

Taking the revolver from the man who'd picked up the weapon, Longarm tucked it into his belt as he nodded his thanks. Then he went on. "Now if you men will sorta edge

7

away so's I'll have enough room to move around, I'll get on with my job."

Reluctantly, the men closest to the corpse began pressing backward, and those who formed the group's bulk gave way bit by bit. Longarm thanked them with a nod and hunkered down in the cleared space that had formed around the sprawled body of the dead man. He dug into the pockets of the outlaw's leather vest, but found only the shredded remains of what had once been two or three cigars in one of the upper pockets and a few matches in the other.

A half-dozen revolver cartridges came out of the lower pockets, together with some scraps of newspaper clippings so torn up and wadded that the print on them was almost unreadable. Longarm decided to defer trying to read them until later. He tucked them away in one of his shirt pockets, then moved to examine the dead man's trouser pockets.

Forcing his hands into them was more difficult, but also more rewarding. Longarm extracted a bulging leather wallet from the first hip pocket he explored, but the other hip pocket yielded only a crumpled bandana. Squeezing his hand into the side pockets he brought out a handful of coins from one, a mixture of silver dollars and gold pieces, while the other pocket contained a clasp-knife and a few more rounds for the pistol. Dumping everything he'd taken from all the pockets into the bandana, he tucked it into the capacious pocket of his coat. Then Longarm stood up and flicked his eyes over the crowd that had formed around him.

"Well, now," he said, "I reckon I've got enough to start on. You men can carry him on down to whatever place it was you said had the coffins—a furniture store, wasn't it?"

"Swenson's," one of the onlookers volunteered. "It's just a little ways down the street from here."

"It'll do for the time being," Longarm said. "You tell whoever runs the place that I'll stop by and have a word with 'em if I can find time before I got to catch my train. And tell 'em that in case I don't have a chance to get there, they can send the bill for burying him to the U.S. marshal's office in Denver."

"You mean the government'll pay to bury him?" one of the men in the little group asked.

"Not hardly," Longarm replied. He held up the bulging bandana he was holding. "But whenever we get a dead outlaw on our hands, there's generally enough money in his pockets to pay for putting him away, so I guess you could say he's paying for his own funeral."

As soon as he'd stepped away from the dead man, the spectators became engrossed in forming a group to carry the outlaw's corpse, while Longarm moved to the bar. Without waiting to be asked, the barkeep filled a shotglass and slid it across the mahogany to Longarm.

"On the house, Marshal," he said.

"Well, thanks," Longarm replied. "A drink always goes down pretty good after I get out of a dustup."

"You know, I had my doubts about that dead fellow when he first come in," the barkeeper went on. "That was before you showed up, but even when you wasn't here he acted like he was sorta nervous. Then I noticed after you come in that he was real careful to keep his back to you, like he was afraid you might recognize him. After a while he slipped out to the street, then he started shooting."

"I got a feeling that I oughta know him," Longarm said with a frown. He downed a swallow from the shotglass, put the glass on the bar, and took one of his long cigars from his pocket. He puffed the cigar alight and held it in his jaws for a moment, then shook his head. "And it ain't real often that I miss out on remembering a face that I've maybe just seen a time or two on a wanted poster. But I sure can't put a name to him."

"You mean there wasn't anything that had his name in that wad of papers I saw you fishing out of his pockets?" the barkeep asked.

Before he'd finished speaking, Longarm was groping in his capacious coat pocket for the papers the barkeep's question had reminded him of. He opened the folded leather wallet first, and saw at a glance that he needed to look no further. The address on the half-folded envelope nestled in the wallet read, "John Larn, X Bar X Ranch, Buffalo, Wyoming."

"Thanks, friend," Longarm said to the barkeep. "I'd likely have remembered to look at what I took outa that dead fellow's pocket, but I'm sure glad I looked when I did. Now, I got another job to do before I can finish that drink, so if you'll just set it on your back bar, I'll finish it later."

Longarm was halfway to the door before he'd finished speaking. He pushed through quickly, leaving the batwings swinging, and hastened along the street, peering anxiously ahead through the gathering darkness. In a moment he saw the half-dozen men who were making slow progress along the unpaved street carrying the body of the dead outlaw, three men on each side of the unwieldy burden.

"Hold on for a minute there, you men!" Longarm called. "I got something important to do!"

When the men carrying their clumsy burden stopped, Longarm walked a bit faster until he came abreast of them.

"What's wrong?" one of the group asked.

"Not a thing I know of," Longarm replied. "After you men left I just got a hunch that I need to take one more look at that dead fellow to make sure I'm right about him being who I think he is. Suppose you lay him down here while I do that."

"Right here in the middle of the street?" one of the body-bearers asked.

"It sure ain't likely that somebody's going to be coming along for the next minute or two," Longarm replied, gesturing toward the totally vacant area around them. "And it won't take but a minute."

Though the faces of the body-carriers bore expressions ranging from questioning to total indifference, the men obeyed Longarm's suggestion. One of them had pulled the edge of a blanket over the dead man's face. Now Longarm lifted the improvised shroud and slipped a match from his pocket. Then he flicked his thumbnail across the head of the match and held it close to the dead face of the corpse while he stared at the outlaw's features. As the match flickered and died away he nodded his head and replaced the covering blanket to hide the face once more.

"I've seen all I need to," he said. "You might tell them fellows who'll be putting him away that his name's John Larn—leastwise, that's the name I saw under a picture of him on a wanted poster we got about him in Denver."

"Larn?" one of the body-bearers said. "I don't recall I ever heard it before. Are you sure he's some kind of outlaw?"

"He was the last time I heard about him, and he was when I got a good look at him one time when he was in jail in Denver on a murder and cattle-rustling charge," Longarm said. "He was sporting a bunch of side-whiskers then, but that don't change his nose and his head. It's Larn, all right."

"Well, you're the man who ought to know," another of the men said.

Longarm nodded. "Now, I got to go back to the saloon before anyone who saw what happened gets away. I'll need to take statements and suchlike to give my chief, so if any

11

of you men saw the blowup, I'd take it kindly if you'd come back and talk to me for a few minutes after you get this body off your hands."

Only one of the corpse-bearers spoke up. He said, "I guess I seen as much of your fracas as anybody, Marshal. I'll be glad to go over it for you if it'll help. Besides, the barkeep promised us a free drink."

"I'll be looking for you then," Longarm told him. "Now, I got to be moving along, or I won't get my job done in time to catch the train I'm waiting for."

Chapter 2

"Oh, the fellow I cut down was Johnny Larn, all right, Billy," Longarm assured Chief Marshal Vail. They were sitting in Vail's private office in the Denver Federal Building. "I found enough papers, letters and bills and stuff, in his wallet to prove that."

"As long as you're sure," Vail told him. "But I don't want to put in my report to the brass in Washington that they can scratch Larn's name off the wanted list and then later on have him pop up someplace."

"He'd just have one place to pop up out of, and that's where the hell-and-damnation bunch winds up going," Longarm said. "Because he sure won't make it to the Pearly Gates. And while we're talking about Larn, when I was going through what few papers were on him, I found out he had a wife over in Texas. She lives in a little town called Albany. Maybe you better tell the clerk to send her anything out of her husband's pockets that we don't need to keep for evidence that'll prove who he was."

"I'll take care of it," Vail said. "And I'll be glad to see Larn's name off our wanted list. We've got enough cases piled up to keep us busy for the next two years."

Longarm was lighting one of his long thin cigars while Vail spoke. When he was satisfied it was drawing properly he took it out of his jaws and asked, "Am I wrong, Billy, or is what you just said a sorta hint that I ain't going to have some time off?"

"I guess you could say it was a hint," Vail answered. "But I won't waste any breath getting down to hard facts." He paused thoughtfully for a moment. "If I recall rightly, you've heard me talk about Matt Carey?"

"I've heard you call his name more'n once. And I met him more'n once. He's that old friend of yours from the war, the one you talked into signing up for a marshal's job when things settled down after the fighting stopped."

"That's right," Vail said. "We swap a letter now and again, and it hasn't been too long since I mentioned you to him. That was right after you took Stang and Cleaver off our wanted list with that shootout up in Wyoming Territory."

"Why, that wasn't such a much of a fracas, Billy. You and me both know that."

"Whether it was or wasn't, it seems to've stuck in Matt's mind," Vail went on. "And right now he's working a big case out in his district. I had a letter from him the other day, and it gave me the idea he feels like it's got too many strings for him to hold onto."

"Now, just a minute, Billy!" Longarm protested. "If you're heading the way I think you are, you're about to tell me that case of Matt Carey's is one you figure to send me out on. And if it is, I ain't even going to be here in Denver long enough to get my laundry done!"

"You just might be right about that," Vail said. "But if it'll make you feel any better, you just might be saving Matt's job if I get you out there to give him the help he's asking for. Otherwise, he's likely to lose his badge besides

14

being up to his belly button in big trouble."

"I'd say that sounds real serious," Longarm declared. "What sort of a jackpot has he got into?"

"Somehow or other, Matt's let about a half-million dollars in United States gold pieces that belong to the Treasury get away from him."

Longarm noticed that the coal at the tip of his cigar was fading to gray, and he puffed at the cheroot for a moment to bring it back to full life before he spoke. After the thin veil of smoke thinned, he stared at Vail for a moment. Then he said, "Maybe I better ask you if I was hearing right, Billy. You did say a half-million dollars, didn't you?"

"Oh, you heard the figure right. And it's not paper money either. That half-million is in gold double eagles. I guess you can work out what that means," Vail said.

"It ain't hard to figure. If it was greenbacks that're missing, all the Treasury clerks would need to do is send out a list of the serial numbers on the bills, send it to all the banks in the country. Then, when one of the bills gets to a bank, they'd spot the number and find out where it was spent. They'd pass the word to the Secret Service, and they'd get busy looking for whoever spent it."

"Exactly," Vail agreed. "But gold pieces don't have numbers like paper money does. Just lately, I've heard there's talk of putting some kind of mark on them so they can tell which mint it was that stamped 'em out. That'd give us some kind of place to start from, but the way it is now all we've got is what the little boy shot at."

"I don't guess that's neither here nor there," Longarm said. "Suppose you start from the beginning and tell me how your friend let that whopping big bunch of double eagles get away from him."

Vail sat silently for a moment while a thoughtful frown flicked over his face. Then he began. "This case goes back

15

a bit, and there's a lot of blank places in it."

"Suppose you fill 'em in, Billy," Longarm suggested.

"Well, the sacks of double eagles were sent from the mint in San Francisco to the marshals' offices in the towns they were going to, just like we used to get them here to deliver to the Denver banks."

"I understand about that, Billy," Longarm said. "If you'll recall, I joined up here before the mint stopped having us deliver the bags. I've toted a few of those sacks myself."

"I don't recall us having to handle a shipment as big as this one, though," Vail said. "There was a half-million dollars worth of double eagles in each shipment when they left the mint. One shipment went to the Oregon capital— that's Eugene—the other one to Grant's Pass, and I'm sure you know where it is."

Longarm frowned. "I'm not real familiar with that part of the country, Billy. Though I've worked more'n one case in those parts."

"I'm not trying to give you a geography lesson, Long," Vail said. His voice was a bit snappish. "All I'm out to do is explain the case you're going out on."

"Sure," Longarm said. "But I don't see how you can dot every i and cross every t right here and now. From the way you started out, I get the idea that something happened to those gold coins on their way to the banks. Am I right?"

"Halfway right," Vail replied. "Like I just said, both shipments were delivered to the marshals' offices. But now one of them's disappeared."

Longarm nodded. "I figured it might be something like that. Which one of the shipments was it?"

"It was the one tagged for Grant's Pass, Matt Carey's office."

"You're sure the other shipment's still where it oughta be?"

"I sent a wire to Cliff Warner, asking him," Vail replied unhesitatingly. "He wired back that the gold left with him was safe and sound."

"And from the way you been putting things, I reckon you're sending me out there to help Matt Carey get out of his jackpot?"

"If you want to put it that way, the answer's yes," Vail said. "And if it makes you feel any better, Cliff's more than ready to get you out there to give Matt a hand."

"From what you said, I take it to mean you asked him?"

"Damn it, Long! You ought to know that I wouldn't butt into another man's jurisdiction unless I was invited! I'd see if he wanted help, or needed some, before I said anything."

"You found out how Cliff felt then?"

"Of course I did!" Vail snapped. Then in a calmer voice he went on. "A day or so after I got Cliff Warner's wire saying the gold in his office was safe, I got another telegram saying he'd like to have some help for Matt Carey. Cliff being chief marshal, any trouble Matt gets into is bigger trouble for Cliff."

"So Cliff came right out and asked for you to help Matt?" Longarm asked.

"Well, Cliff and me, we go back a long ways," Vail said. "He wouldn't pull any punches, he'd tell me about whatever trouble he's likely to get in. If you want the real facts of the matter, I got the idea from his wire that he'd be right glad to see somebody from outside of his jurisdiction come in on the case. Likely it'd save a lot of the trouble he'd be in for when the big brass in Washington finds out about all that lost gold."

Longarm nodded, then sat in silence for a moment before asking, "Billy, just what in tunket do you figure for me to do when I get out to Oregon?"

"You know as well as I do the shipment of gold double eagles didn't just grow a set of legs and walk away under its own steam," Vail replied. "Somebody—likely two or three somebodies—had to carry it out."

"So what you're looking for me to do is team up with Matt Carey to run down whoever it was that done the carrying."

"And give Matt a hand getting back the gold," Vail added quickly.

"That goes without saying," Longarm told him. "I guess you'll expect me to leave yesterday?"

"You know I don't like to push one of my deputies, Long," Vail said. "And I'm not forgetting that you just got back from a case that meant doing some long traveling. I had the clerk put some sleeping-coach vouchers in, and told him to be sure you'd have enough expense money."

"Well, now, all that's right thoughtful of you, Billy. I wouldn't exactly say you're pushing me, but even if you did push a mite, I ain't one to do a lot of complaining."

"I'll give you credit for that, Long," Vail said. "But this case isn't like most of the ones we get. Damn it, that gold was stolen from one of our own offices! We're going to have to find it and recover it as fast as we can, or everybody's going to be saying the Marshals' force is full of jackasses wearing badges. We need to move fast and find the gold, arrest whoever stole it, and get 'em behind bars!"

"Why, I figured right off that was where you were heading for, Billy," Longarm said. "And you know I ain't about to lallygag. Now, there's a few little chores I got to take care of before I start out, like seeing to my laundry and getting the cobbler to fix up the heels on my working boots, but before tomorrow's over with, I'll be on the night train heading west."

● ● ●

Longarm shifted his position on the uncomfortable Pullman car seat, making perhaps his twentieth effort to find a spot that was not bumpy or steel-hard. As had been the case each time he'd sought greater comfort before, he failed to find a spot where he could settle down without feeling that he was sitting on bare boards. The Pullman car was sparsely filled, only a dozen seats were occupied, and he'd tried shifting to one of the many vacant ones without success; each seat he'd tried had seemed as hard as the one ticketed to him.

Hour after hour had passed while the train chugged steadily across the desert, a vast and changeless area of sunbaked soil void of all vegetation. The sterile, almost vegetation-free, desert took in a good part of western Utah Territory and pushed into the southern part of Idaho, as well as making a sizeable bite across Oregon's southeastern boundary to dip into the northernmost fringes of California.

Now the slowly moving wave of darkness that had begun creeping across the featureless land in the half-completed sunset was beginning to hide the landscape's alien look. The dimness of oncoming night was veiling the continuing monotony of sandy soil dotted only with an occasional clump of pale-green cactus struggling to survive in a virtually waterless land.

Everywhere the hard-baked surface of the nearly white earth looked as though it would be equally unfriendly to both man and beast as Longarm gazed at it from the coach window. Occasionally he stole a glance across the aisle at a young woman, but her face was always turned away from him, her eyes fixed on the mostly featureless landscape.

The sun had just set completely when a tinkle of chimes sounded from the front of the coach. Longarm looked around and saw a young boy dressed like a waiter beginning to approach down the aisle. After he'd taken several steps the youth stopped and called, "Dinner's on in the dining car up ahead. And there won't be no second call, so if any of you folks are hungry, you better go on and get a place at a table before all the seats is filled."

Even before the boy had started back toward the rest of the train, the young woman had left her seat and hurried forward. Longarm stood up and stepped into the aisle, realizing that if he did not hurry he'd be stuck in a waiting line as the passengers hastened to the diner. The young woman was now nearing the front vestibule and Longarm glanced back, seeing that most of the passengers from the rear seats were now moving toward him. He took longer steps, and managed to get behind the young woman just before the aisle was flooded with other passengers. Without trying to speak to her Longarm followed her to the vestibule. The door to the dining car had not yet been opened. Longarm stopped behind her.

While he'd been securing his position in the waiting line the young woman had not glanced over her shoulder. Now she twisted her head to look at the line of passengers which had already formed behind them. Other passengers were now coming in from the rest of the train. As she turned back from her quick inspection she said to Longarm, "It looks like we got here just in time."

"Well, it generally pays to be quick on the trigger," he replied. Then through the glass pane in the vestibule door he glimpsed a waiter coming toward them. "If you ain't got no objections, ma'am, we can take that first table in the dining car, just inside the door. That way we can get out fast as we're getting in after we finish eating."

"That's a very good idea," she agreed. "Now, since we're going to sit together, perhaps we'd better introduce ourselves. My name is Idana Kirk."

"I'm right pleased to make your acquaintance, ma'am. Mine's Long, Custis Long."

Before they could go on with their conversation, the door to the vestibule door was opened by one of the dining-car attendants. Longarm and Idana moved quickly into the car and took the seats beside the window while the people behind them pushed ahead. They were just getting settled when a waiter came up and removed the chairs that filled the space between their seats and the aisle.

"I'll be right back to take your orders," he said. "There's a party of six up ahead that wants to sit together. But if you want to order now, I might as well tell you that you just need to say whether you want roast beef or fried chicken."

Longarm and Idana spoke at the same time, each of them ordering roast beef. The waiter nodded and left, carrying the chairs. A moment of awkward silence followed before Idana broke it by saying, "At least we'll have room to eat comfortably."

"Well, trains have got a way of being crowded," Longarm said. "But I got to ride 'em pretty much in my line of work."

"What kind of work do you do?"

"I'm a deputy United States marshal."

"Why, I'd never have known it to look at you."

"Oh, us marshals don't have any uniforms or folderol like that. And like my chief in the office I work out of says, any lawman that tips off a crook is a fool."

"Which office is that, Marshal Long?"

"Denver. But I reckon I spend more time going out on cases than I do in the office."

"Are you on a case now?" Idana asked. Then she shook her head. "Or shouldn't I ask questions like that?"

"Oh, I'm setting out on a case," Longarm answered. "But I ain't supposed to tell folks what it concerns."

"I should've known that," she said with a smile. "Perhaps we'd better talk about the weather or something as harmless."

During their brief meal Longarm and Idana actually talked very little. They ate hurriedly, for the crowd of passengers waiting to be served was already pushing into the dining car. Their dinner eaten, they started back to the Pullman coach, and as they entered it saw its aisle was lined with the green curtains which told them that their berths had been made ready.

"Looks like we ain't got much to do but turn in," Longarm commented. "So I reckon all we can do is say good night."

"Well, I've enjoyed your company, Marshal Long. And I'm sure we'll have other times to chat before our trip is over. But since it seems that we don't have any choice but to turn in, I suppose that's what we'd better do."

While she was still speaking Idana had stopped beside one of the curtained berths. For a moment Longarm did not realize that it was directly across from his own. When he did, he said, "It looks like we're neighbors too."

"And I'll feel very safe, knowing that there's an officer of the law so close." While she was speaking, Idana was parting the green drapes of her bunk. Just as she stepped between its folds and disappeared, she added, "Good night, Marshal Long."

"Good night, ma'am," he replied, then pulled aside the drapes of his berth and bent to settle down on his own bunk.

Longarm closed the thick green curtains. Though pulling them together had dimmed the light in the small enclosure, he began getting ready to turn in even before his eyes had adjusted to the dimness. He'd seen that whoever had been responsible for preparing the berths had hung his hat on

22

the clothes hook at the edge of the bunk. Now he removed the hat and placed it on a pillow before unbuckling his gunbelt and dropping his holstered revolver on the narrow bunk beside the hat.

By twisting and turning a bit he got his coat off and hung it on the clothes hook. Then he sat down long enough to lever his boots off, step out of his trousers, and shrug off his shirt after unbuttoning it. He hung the garments on the hook over his coat, then hung his gunbelt carefully on top of the clothing.

Longarm spent a moment adjusting the gunbelt's position on the garment hook, making sure the holstered Colt's butt would be within easy reach of his hand. Then he skinned out of his light summer underwear and draped it over the other garments on the hook, taking pains to tuck its sleeves and legs behind the clothing already on the hook to insure that he'd have no trouble in grasping the Colt's butt by raising his hand a few inches.

Satisfied at last that he'd taken all the necessary precautions, Longarm stretched out on the bunk atop the folded bed clothing, and settled down for the night. The regular clicking of the Pullman car's wheels on the small expansion cracks of the rails, where their steel ends butted together, reached his ears like a tiny rhythmic lullaby, and Longarm was ready for sleep.

He'd reached the state of dozing with half-closed eyes that comes in the moments just before full slumber arrives when he saw the green curtains shake in a tiny ripple. For a moment, he stared at the curtains, thinking that he'd been deceived by some sort of illusion in the semi-darkness of the berth, until a ripple shook the curtains for a second time.

Now Longarm was sure of what he'd seen. Moving cautiously but swiftly, he reached for the Colt's butt. He had the pistol in his hand, and was swinging it to level at the berth's masking curtains when Idana Kirk's face rose above the edge of the berth. When she saw the threatening muzzle of the revolver only inches from her face, her eyes flew open wide and she began to shake her head.

"No, Marshall Long!" she gasped. Her voice was low, a mere husky whisper. "For heaven's sake, don't shoot me! I certainly didn't come here to harm you!"

Idana had continued lifting herself to her knees as she spoke, and now she raised her arms to show Longarm that her hands were empty.

"I'm sure sorry I surprised you," Longarm said as he laid his Colt aside. "But when a man's got a job like mine, there's almost always somebody ready to gun him down, regardless of wherever he might be. Now, if you come for what I hope you're after, you're welcome as the flowers in May. Just stretch out your hand, and I'll help you finish getting in here with me."

Chapter 3

Idana raised her arms to reach for Longarm's extended hand. He levered her to her feet, and for a moment she stood motionless. She was wearing only a thin white silken nightgown that was almost transparent. In the dim glow filtering into the berth from the night lights at each end of the coach her body seemed to be a moving, shimmering white pillar.

Longarm's eyes had already adjusted themselves to the dimness. Now, as he gazed at Idana, he could see through the thin fabric of her gown and could make out the pink budded bosom spots at the tips of her full breasts and the dark triangle of her pubic brush. Idana stood motionless: she did not seem to be at all embarrassed by his prolonged scrutiny, nor did she change her expression when she saw that Longarm was naked and already beginning an erection.

"I hope you won't object to me making the first move," Idana said after a moment or two had slipped away. "But I've been turning and tossing in that berth across the aisle ever since I lay down on it. I was sure that I'd go right off to sleep."

"But you weren't all that sleepy?" Longarm asked.

"Not after I got to thinking about you being alone over here and me being alone in my own berth. That's when I began trying to decide whether or not to join you, and—well, I don't suppose I need to go any further."

"I sorta had you on my mind too," Longarm admitted. "I didn't make a move because I figured just about like you did, that you might not be of a mind to make me feel exactly at home if I were to try getting into your berth."

"I had pretty much the same feeling, wondering if you'd welcome me," Idana confessed. "Then I got itchier and itchier while I was realizing that you were too much of a man to object and that the night wasn't going to last forever. Now that I can see you're getting ready to welcome me, I'm very glad that I came across the aisle."

"Well, now," Longarm said. "We know we got the same thing on our mind, so let's don't waste any more time palavering."

Before Longarm had finished speaking, Idana was moving to follow his suggestion. She shrugged out of her transparent silken nightgown, letting it fall to the floor as she moved closer to him. Their bodies brushed together, and when Longarm bent to find her lips, she met his out thrust tongue with hers as their opened lips pressed together. While they were entwining tongues, their hands began exploring one another. Longarm was caressing Idana's jutting breast-blossoms while she grasped his jutting erection and slid it between her thighs.

Longarm held her for a few moments with an arm around her back and his other hand cradling her buttocks to support her wriggling body as he shifted their position to get Idana's back toward the bed. She'd been caressing his crotch, and now she placed him. Locking her legs around his hips, she drew herself toward him.

26

Longarm felt her moist warmth engulfing him, but he did not move when Idana slipped her arms up to his shoulders and clasped her hands behind his back. For a moment or two he was motionless while holding her suspended. He did not try to thrust more deeply, but turned and twisted and shuffled his feet to be sure that Idana would land safely on the narrow Pullman bed. Then he let himself fall forward, carrying her with him, and as her back landed on the narrow bed he thrust, driving fully into her with a single swift lunge.

Idana gasped when Longarm's penetration drove home. Then she loosed a long drawn-out and almost silent cry of pleasure when Longarm held himself motionless for a few moments. She locked her legs around his hips just before he began stroking with slow measured drives. At the apex of each thrust he pressed to her, holding himself buried deeply for a short while.

When Idana's body started to shiver mildly Longarm changed his tempo to a faster pace, bracing his knees on the thin mattress. He kept driving with closely spaced but deliberate thrusts, each one as deep and lusty as the one that had preceded it. Idana caught his rhythm quickly, and started arching her back upward to bring her buttocks high at the apex of each deep drive, twisting her hips in a continuous rolling motion as she held him fully buried.

After the first few moments of driving fast and fully, Longarm slowed the tempo of his closely spaced thrusts to a slower pace. Again Idana caught his rhythm, and changed the upward movements of her hips to match it. She'd clasped her arms behind his back, but with the slower tempo Longarm was now setting she could release one arm to reach up and pull Longarm's head down. As their lips met she slipped her tongue into Longarm's mouth, and he met it with his own.

Now the meeting of their lips and the entwining of their tongues led them to a slower rhythm for Longarm's body-shaking penetrations. Longarm maintained his steady pace of thrust and lift until he felt Idana's body begin to twitch in the first tremors of consummation. Now Longarm slowed the tempo of his lusty downward strokes even more. When he reached the apex of a thrust he pushed his hips more firmly against hers, pinning her to the bunk's thin mattress, holding himself deeply buried.

For a short time they both lay motionless. Then Idana twisted her hips furiously. Longarm understood her signal and began to drive again. Soon Idana's body began quivering, and now Longarm speeded the tempo of his lunges. He drove into her steadily while minute by minute the quivers that had begun to ripple through Idana's form became more closely spaced. Within what seemed a very short time she was bucking her hips furiously, shaking spastically and beginning to gasp. After several more minutes Longarm started to quiver at the end of each stroke, a signal that he knew was foretelling full consummation.

He speeded the rhythm of his lunges once more. Only moments after he'd done so Idana loosed a small throaty cry. Her shudders accelerated and she started rotating her hips at an even faster pace. Longarm matched her new moves and released his own control, and before he'd lunged a dozen times to bury himself deeply, his own body began to quiver.

Suddenly Idana tightened her arms around him and held herself to him. Longarm's jerking spasms had increased swiftly after he began his final drive. He felt Idana's hips bucking and twisting and drove faster. After a few moments, Idana began raising her hips in a constant succession of lifting heaves to the accompaniment of a small stream of soft bubbling cries. Again Longarm bent to kiss her, and Idana met his tongue with hers as he thrust it between her lips.

With their tongues entwined, their quivering forms no longer twisted furiously as Longarm jetted to match Idana's flow. Now they lay quiescent, Longarm no longer driving, Idana's movements limited to an occasional spastic shudder. Then even the shudders faded and stopped. Longarm sagged to rest as they lay motionless and fully spent.

Longarm was the first to recover. His voice was unusually soft as he murmured into Idana's ear, "It sorta seems like we get along pretty good."

"Better than good," she told him. "I'd say marvelous. I've been living like an old maid for the past three or four months, since my husband left me. I really needed to bed down with a man like you."

"Well, all I can say is that I'm as glad to've run into you as you were to meet up with me. Now, we might be a little bit crowded in this narrow berth, but why don't we just lay right like we are now for a while and rest a bit."

"Am I wrong, or do you mean you can do it again?"

"Why, I guess I got another go or two left in me. That is, if you feel up to it."

"Oh, don't worry about that. I've never been in bed with a man like you before, and I don't want to say good night or good-bye any sooner than we'll have to."

"Well, there ain't no reason to be jumping off that bridge till we get to it," Longarm replied. "So let's just put off saying our good-byes till we got to, and make the night last as long as we can."

Standing beside his travel gear on the depot platform in Grant's Pass, Longarm waved good-bye to Idana Kirk. She'd come out to the the vestibule platform of the last car, and was fluttering her handkerchief in farewell while the train that was carrying her north pulled away from the

29

station and vanished around a curve in the tracks.

As soon as Idana's waving handkerchief was no longer visible, Longarm picked up his rifle and the valise on which it had been leaning. He started toward the two-story brick building across the street, for he'd noticed when he stepped off the train that it had a sign reading "Post Office" on its facade. Above the sign, on the second floor, there was a pair of wide windows, one of them bearing in gilt letters the legend "U.S. Marshal."

Inside the building, Longarm wasted only a glance at the postal workers who were sorting letters and stuffing them into the array of pigeonholes that filled the wall beyond the counter. He saw the stairway at the end of the post office windows, and mounted its steps two at a time in spite of the burden of his suitcase and rifle.

All but one of the doors dotting the narrow second-floor corridor were closed. The exception was at the end of the hall, where a door with an upper panel of translucent glass stood slightly ajar. The lettering "U.S. Marshal" was clearly visible, and without stopping to knock, Longarm pushed the door open and went in.

He stopped just inside the door and discovered that the room he'd entered was surprisingly spacious but its furnishings were sparse. There was a battered oak desk at one end, its surface bare except for a small triangular wooden plaque that bore the legend "Deputy U.S. Marshal M. Carey." A half-dozen chairs lined the wall beside the entry door, and a trio of battered wooden file cases nestled against the rear wall.

A man was hunkered down in front of one of the file cases. His back was toward the hall door, and when he heard Longarm come in he swiveled around. A smile crinkled the man's tanned face as he stood up and stepped to the doorway, extending his hand to grasp Longarm's.

"Well, all I got to say is, you taken your time getting here," he said as they shook hands. "I been looking for you damn near every day since Cliff Warner let me know you was coming to give us a hand. And now that you finally made it, I reckon I'm glad to see you."

"Why, I'm real glad to see you again, Matt," Longarm assured him. "But I'm just about as glad to get my feet onto some real ground that ain't moving all the time. It seems like to me that I was on that damn train long enough for it to take me plumb to Alaska."

"Well, if you're not too tired of setting to be comfortable, come on over and we'll set down and talk by my desk," Carey suggested. As he started walking beside Longarm he went on. "It ain't that I'm trying to push you, Longarm. Thing is, Cliff said I oughta not waste any time getting you started, seeing that this case is all tangled up with our outfit."

"Now you're putting the cart before the horse," Longarm replied. "I got to admit, all I know about things out here is that there's a hell of a big bunch of double eagles missing. And the last place anybody knows about 'em being is right here in your office."

While they talked the two men had been walking slowly across the room toward the desk. Carey gestured for Longarm to take the chair beside it, and settled himself into the one behind the sign that bore his name.

"Then you know as much about them double eagles as I do myself," Carey admitted. "Them damned bags got here on a Saturday. The train was running late, and the messengers from San Francisco didn't stay long. Most all the trains that go through here is just locals, because the town ain't on the main line."

"Now, hold on," Longarm said. "How come I got here without changing from the train I got on at Salt Lake?"

31

"Well, I guess you was lucky, Longarm," Carey replied. "The damn railroad bought up the tracks and right-of-way from an outfit that didn't have no call to be in railroading in the first place. They was supposed to lay rails from San Francisco to Portland, but they run out of money before they got all the way to Portland."

"I still don't get the drift of what you're trying to tell me," Longarm said.

"That's because I'm not finished yet. The California Northern had the right-of-way, but they didn't find out first that if they wanted to keep it they'd have to run trains on it, because if they didn't their rights wouldn't mean diddly-squat. No trains, no right-of-way."

"I'm running ahead of you now," Longarm said when Carey paused for breath. "The company went bust and sold out."

"Why, sure," Carey said. "They didn't have no way to get trains to it, but the S.P. did, so they struck a deal for the S.P. to buy 'em out. The S.P. runs three trains a week from their main line up here, mostly just to keep their right-of-way alive till they get finished laying track up north."

"I get the drift now," Longarm said when Carey paused for breath. "But let's get back to that shipment of double eagles."

"You know, it's a sorta funny thing, Longarm. Nobody's ever told me why U.S. Marshals gets those shipments of new money, which we then got to deliver to the banks."

"Oh, Billy Vail told me how that come about," Longarm said. "Right after the San Francisco mint got going—and that'd be a good while back—it wasn't what you'd call easy to send the money it'd started turning out to towns where a lot of little banks needed it. So the mint started dropping money shipments off at the U.S. Marshals' offices the Justice Department had already set up, and the marshals

32

got the job of delivering it around."

"That sure sounds like a hell of a way to run a mint," Carey observed. "I've worked at a lot of hay-barn towns, but I never did run into that kind of a job before I got transferred down here."

"Well, we were still looking after mint shipments when I got started in Denver," Longarm told him. "But Billy Vail didn't like the idea of us doing what's a job for the mint. I guess this might be about one of the few places left where they still do it."

"Now that you mention Billy, I guess he was the one who sent you out here."

"That's about the size of it," Longarm said. "But don't forget it was Cliff Warner that officially asked him to send me."

"Oh, I already knew that. What I'm wondering now is how you're going to start."

"Why, I'm starting right now," Longarm answered. "What I'm wondering is how much help you can give me."

"I'll give you all the help I can, but don't look for me to tell you something I don't know much about myself."

"If you'll recall, Matt, I don't put much store in paper clues. When you're standing up to a man and looking him in the eye, you can tell right quick whether he's lying or telling the truth. You sure won't get help like that from a sheet of paper that can't look you in the eye and talk back to you."

"It seems I've heard you say something to that effect before," Carey said. "So just remember that I ain't turned my head away from you yet."

"Why, I didn't look for you to, and I still don't. Now, go on and tell me what you can about those bags of double eagles."

Carey was silent for a moment, then he shook his head. "There's just not anything I can tell you about them, Longarm. The only time I got a look at the bags was when the fellows from the San Francisco mint delivered them. They opened them up and stood by while I made a quick count of the double eagles. It was easy to do, because they was still wrapped up in rolls of ten in them heavy brown-paper wrappers, just like they always are when the mint ships 'em."

"Did your tally come out all right?"

"Oh, sure. I prised open the end of three or four of the rolls, mostly because the messengers asked me to make sure. The tally was right to a T, so I tucked the bags away in a locker, like I'd got in the habit of doing. Then I signed the delivery receipt and the mint fellows left."

"And that was the last time you had anything to do with the bags?" Longarm asked.

"Well, sure. If anybody'd broke into them, I'd've seen the signs of what they'd done. Oh, I opened the locker every day or so, just to make sure."

"But you didn't open up the bags when you opened the locker?"

"Why, there wasn't any reason to," Carey replied. "If there'd been anybody come into the office here and messed with those bags, I'd've noticed it. After whoever it was broke in, all I had to do was look around to figure out what had happened."

"I reckon you told the postmaster downstairs that somebody'd busted in up here," Longarm said.

"Well, Longarm, I felt like I had to tell the postmaster, on account of him being in charge of the building. But I asked him to keep quiet about it to his help, because I didn't figure it'd do neither one of us much good if the word was spread around town that a burglar'd busted into the place."

"You didn't send anything out on the telegraph wire either, I guess?"

"Why, that'd've been just like me going outside and yelling about what had happened."

"Then you and the postmaster's the only ones in town here that know about the gold pieces being stolen?" Longarm was frowning thoughtfully as he asked the question.

"Far as I know, we are. Unless whoever grabbed that gold has been talking, which I don't reckon'd be likely."

"What about the person who cleans here?"

"There ain't one," Carey answered. "Leastwise, not up here in this office. I sweep out now and then, when I got the time. Except for when somebody comes up here to report some sort of trouble that the local law can't handle, I'm the only one in the office."

"Well, we sure ain't got much to go on," Longarm noted. "I reckon you did tell the sheriff or the constable or whoever's supposed to be the local law?"

Carey shook his head. "Except for sending word to Cliff Warner up in Eugene, I haven't said a word to anybody, Longarm. Except for the people at the bank. I forgot about that. I figured they oughta know. Maybe it wasn't the right thing to do, but it seemed like to me that it was. And I didn't send Cliff a telegraph message. I wrote him a letter."

"Well, now, Matt, I won't say you're wrong and I won't say you're right. There's times when a man in our kind of job don't know whether to jump or squat or just stand still, times when you're damned if you do and damned if you don't. About all I can see to do is prowl around town for a day or so and see what we can dig up. Now, part of the time I'll figure on taking you along with me, and there'll likely be times when I'll be going by myself."

"You mean you've got something in mind already?"

"I reckon you could say I have and I haven't. Tell me more about this bank you just mentioned."

35

"Well, it ain't such a much of a bank. But first thing I did was question everyone who worked there. Without much luck."

"Well, maybe our luck will change. I'd guess it'd be open this time of day?"

"Oh, sure. Fellow by the name of Shaw owns it. He's a funny sort, don't have a lot to say, wears gloves all the time, even when he's indoors, but I reckon he's all right. They stay open till six o'clock, and till noon on Saturdays."

"Let's us be moving then. Like I said, there's times in a case like this when you don't know exactly where to start, but you got to start somewhere and the bank seems to me like it's as good a place as any."

Chapter 4

"I'm sure that all the people employed by my bank have heard about that missing gold, Marshal Long," Alfred Shaw said. "But I expect Marshal Carey's already told you that for a week or more he's been asking questions of everybody who works here."

"Well, now, Matt's told me he's moseyed around a lot and that he's talked some with the folks here at your bank," Longarm said. He and Carey were sitting across from the banker's oversized desk in his private office at the rear of the bank building.

"I'm sure he's asked enough questions to satisfy himself that nobody here in the bank knows anything about those double eagles," Shaw stated. "But even though I think it'd be a waste of time, if you want to ask more questions, I'd be the last man to object."

"Well, him coming here to your bank makes good sense to me," Longarm said. "Seeing as how folks in banks handle money all the time. But Matt says none of 'em in yours has told him anything that'd be much help, so maybe I better start thinking about some new questions that needs to be put to 'em."

"I'm sure you'll find out the same thing he did, that none of the bank's employees know anything about the gold you're so interested in," Shaw said. He was shaking his head now. "And you'll also find out very quickly that you're mistaken if you think that any employee of my bank might've been gossiping outside of working hours about that missing gold shipment."

Longarm had been taking stock of the bank's owner from the moment that Carey had introduced them. The banker was a large wiry man, and to Longarm he had the look of someone who'd spent an early lifetime as a cowhand, though at a first glance his attire would have indicated differently.

He was wearing a dark brown silk suit with a tan tie and pongee shirt that would have made him feel at home in a large city. The single unusual note in his clothing was one Carey had mentioned to Longarm: The banker wore a pair of thin flesh-hued leather gloves which fitted his hands so tightly that at first glance they might have been taken for deeply suntanned skin.

Longarm went on. "And I'd guess you've told 'em not to talk about bank affairs to folks that don't work for you, Mr. Shaw?"

"Even before I opened the doors of this bank for business, I gave my tellers and clerks—all of my employees, in fact— very strict orders that they are not to talk about even our smallest transactions with anyone except others who work for me," the banker replied.

"Since you're the boss here, I reckon they toed the line you set down for 'em?"

"Naturally," Shaw answered. "And since then I've kept warning them from time to time never to take part in any discussions with each other unless the matter they're speaking about has a direct connection with their own jobs and is absolutely essential to our business."

Shaw ended his long statement by reaching for a cedarwood cigar box that was resting on the desk top. He opened its lid and and pushed it toward Longarm, his eyebrows raised in a silent invitation. Longarm shook his head as he raised his hand to show the ash-tipped stogie that he'd been carrying without puffing since entering the bank.

"Thanks, but I'll stick to this one," Longarm said. "It went out while we were talking and I never bothered to put a match to it till now."

He took out a match and flicked its tip into flame with his thumbnail. Then while Shaw was lighting the cigar he'd taken from the box, Longarm continued to look across the match flame past the tip of his own cigar, scrutinizing the banker.

Shaw had a puckered face and thin lips. He was seated in a bulky oversized leather-upholstered chair that made him look even larger than he was. The chair was centered between a massively scaled desk and a table. The two pieces of furniture almost filled the banker's office, a narrow crowded room behind the bank's lobby. There was barely enough knee space for Longarm and Carey to sit comfortably in the chairs they'd chosen from the line of straight chairs standing along the wall facing Shaw's huge highly polished desk.

After he'd made sure his own cigar was drawing properly, the banker went on. "And I've also gotten my employees accustomed to consulting me directly when they receive certain kinds of unusual requests."

"Such as what?" Longarm asked.

"Wouldn't you agree that an unusual request would be

a stranger coming into my bank and asking to exchange a substantial quantity of mint-fresh double eagles for coins of smaller denominations or for silver?"

"You mean that's happened lately, or that it ain't?" Longarm asked.

"I'm certainly not saying it has or hasn't," Shaw answered.

"And you'd do the swap for 'em if they did come in?"

"If the exchange was to be for only a few double eagles, say less than five or six, our tellers wouldn't be apt to question it, even if the person making the exchange had no account here. But if it was an unusually large amount, from a stranger, I'm sure that—well, we'd exercise the same precautions that you or Marshal Carey would."

Longarm nodded. "And has there been such a swap?"

For a moment Shaw did not reply. Then he said, "Very few days go by when we don't handle a substantial number of gold coins in all denominations, Marshal Long. We'll get an ingot now and then, and occasionally even nuggets and dust. This is a small town, and we're the only bank."

"Then maybe it wouldn't be too much trouble for you to find out if the kind of a swap we've been talking about ever got made," Longarm suggested.

"No trouble at all," Shaw agreed. He swiveled in his chair to reach and tug at the ornately embroidered bellpull that hung on the wall behind him. Then he turned back to face Longarm and Carey. "My confidential secretary will be here in a moment, and I'm sure he'll have the records—" He broke off when a discreet tapping sounded on the door panel and he called, "Come in, Wilson."

Shaw's voice had barely died away when the door swung open and a large middle-aged man in a dark suit entered. "You rang, sir?" he asked.

"Yes, of course," Shaw replied curtly. "You're already acquainted with Marshal Carey, and this other gentleman is United States Marshal Long. He's from Denver, come here to work with Marshal Carey in tracking down those stolen gold coins we've been questioned about. Go and get your logbook and gold-exchange ledger. I'm sure you'll be able to answer the questions—at least some of them—they've been asking me."

"Immediately, sir," Wilson replied, turning to the door.

"Very good man, Wilson," Shaw said to Longarm and Carey as his secretary closed the door behind him. "He's careful in his record-keeping. I don't recall having to question the accuracy of his ledgers more than a time or two."

"And you reckon we might come up on something in those ledgers he's gone after?" Longarm asked.

Shaw shrugged instead of replying. "You're not likely to be aware of it, Marshal Long, but we keep two gold ledgers. One of them records our acquisitions, minted coins as well as bars or ingots or nuggets. The other keeps a record of our sale or exchange of gold in any form."

Shaw had barely finished speaking when Wilson returned, carrying two leather-bound volumes. He placed them on the table, opened one, and began turning its pages. Watching Wilson's moving hands, Longarm noticed that the back of his right hand bore an old faded scar that was shaped almost exactly like a fishhook. His glimpse was fleeting; he'd gotten just a glance at the scar when Wilson spoke.

"I'm sure you'll find these in order, sir," Wilson said to Shaw. "If you'll tell me what you're looking for, perhaps I can be helpful."

"Double eagles," Longarm said. "Especially new ones fresh from the mint that somebody might've passed or had changed for small cash."

Shaw gestured to Wilson, who shook his head as he said, "I don't recall having seen any mint-fresh gold coins lately, Marshal Long. Certainly no new double eagles. I'd've been sure to notice them, and I'd also know from the records our tellers keep, because I check them every day at the close of business. You can be sure that I'd remember if we'd gotten any."

"I suppose that answers your questions, Marshal Long," Shaw said. He nodded to Wilson, who left. Then he leaned back in his chair. "Is there anything else?" he asked Longarm.

"I reckon we're wound up here for now."

"Good," said Shaw. "But no need to leave right away. Sit and finish your cigar. You've come from Denver, you say?"

After a few minutes of small talk, Longarm and Carey rose to leave. Shaw followed them out of the office. "I'll be glad to have my people keep their eyes peeled, and report anything unusual," Shaw offered.

"That's real thoughtful of you, Mr. Shaw, and I thank you kindly for helping us out," Longarm said.

"I'm sorry that I couldn't give you any more help than I did," Shaw said as he followed Longarm and Carey through the bank to the outer door. After they'd stepped out to the board sidewalk the banker stopped in the open doorway. "But as I said, I'll have our tellers keep their eyes open for the double eagles you're concerned about and notify Marshal Carey if any turn up in our daily transactions."

"Why, we'd be real grateful to you for doing that," Longarm told him.

Shaw had extended his arm for a final handshake, and Longarm was putting out his own hand, when a rifle's unmistakable high-pitched bark broke the stillness of the deserted street. The rifle slug whistled between the two men, and the air created by the speeding bullet brushed Longarm's face as the lead chunk thudded into the wall of the bank behind them.

Longarm and Carey dropped flat at once, drawing their revolvers as they reached the ground and looking around, trying to locate the source of the shot. From the corner of one of the buildings across the street another shot cracked. Behind them, Shaw's body buckled as the rifle slug tore into him and knocked him back against the door frame.

Facing the direction from which the shot had come, concentrating on finding its exact source, neither Longarm nor Carey realized that the banker had been hit until Shaw's body began to crumple as it slid slowly down the frame of the door and sprawled lifeless on the ground.

Another shot barked from somewhere along the ragged line of buildings that was on the opposite side of the street. This time the slug kicked up a spurt of dust in front of Longarm's face, half-blinding him. Stretched flat an arm's length from Longarm, Matt Carey loosed a shot from his revolver.

"Did you see whoever's shooting?" Longarm asked Carey.

"Not hide nor hair," Carey replied. "I just figured I might be lucky and hit whoever it is over yonder that's picked us out for his target practice."

Longarm's eyes were watering and stinging, and he blinked rapidly, trying to clear them as he searched the deserted street.

His vision cleared a bit as he continued to look for the source of the shots, but the film of moisture that now covered his eyeballs made the buildings across the street appear only as blurred shimmering outlines. Even so, he could see that there was no movement nearby, but just as he was about to give up he got a glimpse of a running man flashing by one of the slitlike spaces that separated the buildings.

Longarm swung his Colt, trying to guess when the sniper's moving form would next be visible in the spaces between the structures. While he was waiting he heard the thunking of galloping horse hooves coming from behind the buildings.

"That bastard's getting away!" he called to Carey. "Can you see him from where you are?"

Before Carey could answer, a babble of sounds came from inside the bank and the patter of feet running toward the door drowned out the hoofbeats. Still blinking his eyes to clear them, Longarm leaped to his feet and started to run across the street.

"You stay here and get that bunch in the bank to take care of the banker," he called over his shoulder. "I want another crack at that damned sniper before he gets outa range!"

Without looking back to see if Carey was moving to obey him, Longarm ran across the graveled street. His vision had cleared completely now, and he kept his eyes moving along the ragged line of widely spaced tumbledown buildings that lined it. But he saw no sign of movement in the gaps between them. He pushed on, even though he knew that his effort was foredoomed to failure.

He ran between two of the ramshackle buildings, only to see railroad tracks ahead, and beyond them open country-side. Boxcars and flatcars were scattered willy-nilly along the tracks.

Longarm realized at once that the gravel ballast between the rails would hold no recognizable hoofprints. He studied the area for several minutes, walking up and down the tracks. Finally he shook his head, knowing that trying to follow the trail of the man who'd loosed the shots at him and Shaw and Carey could turn out to be a long and painstaking job, certainly not one that he could carry out on foot.

Reluctantly, Longarm turned back. He reached the street and started across the wheel-rutted thoroughfare. He frowned when he saw that the board sidewalk in front of the bank was not occupied by the usual crowd of curious onlookers that usually assembled at a scene where there'd been gunplay. Nor was Carey standing guard at the closed doors.

As Longarm reached the bank building, the door swung open and Carey stepped forward to greet him.

"I been looking for you to get back," Carey said. "I guess you know that one of them bullets we managed to duck killed Alfred Shaw."

Looking around, Longarm asked, "Then where in tunket's his body got off to?"

"Some of the men from the bank carried him inside, and one of them went for a doctor soon as the shooting was over with. There wasn't much use in him going, but the doctor come anyhow. He's still inside the bank. He kept trying to do something for Shaw, but I left when I seen it wasn't any use."

"Well, I didn't expect I'd find him in good health when I got back," Longarm replied. "But if I hadn't taken out after that ambusher, he could've put us where the banker is now."

"There's another thing that bothers me," Carey said. He stopped short, frowning. "That Wilson fellow seems to be gone."

"You mean the fellow that acted like he was Shaw's private flunkey?"

"Why, sure," Carey said. "He wasn't around while the doctor was working trying to keep Shaw alive—or I oughta say, bring him back from the dead."

"Did you take a look-see through the bank building here?"

"Not a real good one. I was too busy trying to help the doctor."

"I guess you asked if anybody saw him?"

"Oh, sure. But nobody's seen him or knows where he might be holed up."

"Now, that's real strange," Longarm said. "Maybe we both better go inside and have look-see."

"That'd likely be a good idea," Shaw agreed. "I been trying to figure things out, but the men that work here's all bunched up jabbering just about everyplace where there's a quiet corner. And the doctor's still inside, trying to figure out what to do with Shaw's body."

"Well, now," Longarm went on, "if he's dead, I guess he'll have to be buried, and that's for somebody else to say, not us. But let's go inside and have a little look-see."

Longarm pushed through the entry door and Carey followed. A small group of men, obviously members of the bank's staff, were bunched up at the rear of the room. They were gathered around an elderly man, bending near him and talking in hushed voices.

A shrouded figure lay on a double desk at one side of the room, covered by curtains that had been pulled hastily from a nearby window. Through the curtainless window that was only a short step or two from the desk bright sunlight glared, bathing the desk and its burden in a flood of light.

Longarm stepped up to the desk, reaching for the curtain that covered the banker's motionless form. Turning back to Carey, he said, "Even if I know whose body this is, there'll likely be an inquest or what passes for one in a town out here. I'll just lift up this curtain and take a quick look-see so I can testify."

Lifting the curtain was not easy, for its folds had been tucked under the body of the dead banker. Longarm gave the improvised shroud a quick tug, and as the curtain pulled

46

free the arm of the covered dead man flopped off the desk top and fell dangling over the side of the desk.

Carey loosed a yelp of surprise and recoiled from the desk when the body's hand moved. Longarm stepped back, and as he did so he glanced at the dangling motionless arm. His single quick look told him the reason why the dead banker had worn gloves in his office.

Outlined clearly in the sun's glaring light he saw the tattooed outline of a fishhook on the back of Shaw's hand. Longarm stood staring at the mark, for the moment he'd seen it he realized it was the same pattern as that of the scar on the hand of the missing Wilson.

Chapter 5

"Just step back over here a minute, Matt," Longarm said. When Carey moved up to his side, Longarm went on. "Take a look at Shaw's hand and then tell me what this tattoo on it brings to your mind."

Bending over to get a good look at the dead man's dangling hand, Carey studied the fishhook tattoo for a moment. Then he straightened up and looked at Longarm with a puzzled frown. He started to say something, then bent for another quick glance at the corpse's hand. Then he turned back to Longarm and shook his head.

"Now, I can see real clear that this tattooing's meant to be a fishhook," Carey said. "But that's all I can make out about it, Longarm. Why?"

"Damn it, Matt, you ain't using your head right now except for a place to hang your hat on!" Longarm's voice was uncharacteristically sharp. "Think about it for a minute!"

"Well, maybe before Shaw got to be a big rich banker, he might've worked at being a sailor, or more likely a fisherman," Carey said. "Living all the way back east in

Colorado like you do, I don't reckon you think much about there being a big lot of men out here along the coast that earns a living just by going out fishing every day."

"Oh, I know there's lots of fishing, but that don't make no never-mind," Longarm said. "What I want to know is, don't you remember seeing another mark something like this one?"

Carey started to shake his head. Then his jaw dropped and he exclaimed, "Sure I do, now you remind me of it! That Wilson, the fellow who works in Shaw's office! He's got some sorta mark on his hand that looks a little bit like this!"

"That's right," Longarm said. "It's what popped into my head when I looked at Shaw's hand just now."

"Only Wilson's wasn't quite the same," Carey went on. "As I recall, it wasn't nowheres near as dark, and someways I got the idea that it had sorta been whittled at, like he'd maybe tried to cut the skin off."

"There wouldn't be much of any other way to get rid of it," Longarm noted. "Because there ain't nothing it could be covered up with. What most folks don't think about, or maybe don't even know, is when they get a tattoo mark scribbled on 'em, that mark's going to be there as long as they live."

"Well, I never had a notion to get my hide all hashed up thataway," Carey said. "But I can see now what you've been getting at, Longarm. Tell me if I'm wrong, but if Shaw and Wilson both got the same mark on 'em, I'd take it to mean they must've been together in some kind of outfit that made everybody in it get one of these tattoos put on their hands."

"Now you're ringing the bell loud and clear," Longarm said. "Except that I never ran across a bank or a ranch or a business of any kind that made whoever worked for 'em get all marked up with a sign that couldn't be gotten rid of."

"What you're driving at is that Shaw and Wilson used to be together in some sorta outlaw gang?"

"Not used to be," Longarm said soberly. "My hunch is that likely they still are, or were till Shaw got killed."

Carey shook his head. "That don't seem likely, Longarm. Why, it'd mean they was just sorta putting on a show for us and—"

"If whoever's bossing a gang of crooks is smart enough, he'd figure out some ways to hang onto their loot without burying it. They'd need to find a place that'd be handy to get to when they ran short of ready money. And I can't think of anyplace that'd be better than a bank run by one of their bosses in a little outa-the-way town like this one is. Can you?"

After a moment of thoughtful silence, Carey said, "This town'd suit 'em to a T, all right, and a scheme like that'd be real smart of 'em to use. So what you're saying is that Shaw was head man for a gang of crooks?"

Longarm nodded. "To me it makes good sense. Shaw was the boss and that big Wilson fellow was here to back him up."

"Oh, makes sense to me too now," Carey agreed.

"I'd guess the rest of the outlaws are hiding out somewhere," Longarm said.

"Well, Longarm, I guess I must've been behind the door when brains was being passed out," Carey said, his voice showing his feelings. "But I never did get a hint that anything crooked was going on at the bank."

"Just stop and figure a minute, Matt. Let's say you're an outlaw, but a real smart one, if there is any such thing. You start up a bank in a little town that ain't worth diddly-squat; then, when your outlaw friends need a safe place to

51

hide away whatever cash they've got, you take care of it for 'em."

"You're sure that's what Shaw and Wilson was doing?"

"I'd say it's pretty likely. Look at it this way, Matt. My bet is that Shaw learned from holding up banks that they don't have all that much cash on hand except in paper money. You and me both know how paper money leaves a trail. It's got numbers on it and the numbers can be traced down."

"But hard money don't carry numbers," Carey said. "Except for a mint mark that tells the year it was made. So you decide not to steal paper money, and you just go for what gold the bank's got. If it's a lot, so much the better."

Longarm nodded. "Then you find out about a big bunch of gold close by and easy to get at, so you decide to make a play for it."

"Wait a minute, Longarm!" Carey protested. "If you're getting around to saying that I didn't take good enough care of those sacks of double eagles in my office—"

"No, *you* wait a minute," Longarm broke in, straining not to act too much like a schoolteacher. "Let me finish up what I was starting to get at. That Wilson fellow turning up missing don't mean but one thing to me now. How about you?"

Carey nodded. "He killed Shaw and now he's took tail."

"Now you're taking the peel off the apple!" Longarm said. "So we've figured out now that the two of 'em were in cahoots. And my guess is that Wilson got greedy when he saw a chance to grab those double eagles for himself."

"That's bound to be the way it was," Carey agreed. "And once he'd done it, he'd have to get away real quick."

"I'd say you've got it nailed down solid," Longarm said.

"Then right now, he's heading for a place to lay low," Carey said.

"Exactly. And if him and Shaw didn't already have a hidey-hole set up waiting for 'em, sure as God made little green apples, when Wilson got out there on the railroad tracks, he was heading for some big town where he could put those gold pieces away and be sure they were safe."

"Meaning maybe Medford? It's the only big town to the south."

"Now, that'd be hard to say," Longarm told him. "But I'd figure to go a good ways further on. I'd guess he might even be headed as far away as San Francisco."

"Now that is a hell of a stretch off!" Carey protested.

"So maybe he goes to hole up first," Longarm said. "Now, you've been in this part of the country long enough to learn what sorta hideout an outlaw'd be looking for. Tell me about a few places that come to mind."

"Why, from what I've found out since I was posted here, there ain't none," Carey replied. "From what I've listened to when some of the old-timers get to yarning, this part of Oregon never was much of a place for outlaws, Longarm. Oh, sure, there's been a few, but around here it's not like it is in the gold country, nor in the cattle country either."

"Well, it's been a pretty long spell since I worked my last case out here," Longarm said. "But I figure I can find an outlaw."

"Now hold on, Longarm! Do you figure you know enough about this country to track down a man you just barely got a look at?"

"Maybe I don't know much about the country, but after chasing down outlaws long as I have, I sure do know the kinda places they hole up in. And from what I've learned about 'em, you could spit a wad of tobacco on any map of Oregon and damn near anywhere it leaves a spatter is a place where outlaws could hide out and never be bothered. I reckon you know how heavy gold weighs. If Wilson's got very far to go, he'll stash that gold right here, and plan on coming back to get it when things cool down. Or maybe he had a packhorse close by to put the gold sacks on. That'd make a lot more sense to me."

Carey did not reply for a moment. At last he said thoughtfully, "I guess it does to me too. If it was me, I'd take the gold and cut a shuck for someplace far enough away where I could hide out awhile. Close around town here, there'd be too much chance of somebody stumbling onto them two sacks of gold. But how're we going to find out where he'd head for?"

"Now, Matt, you're acting like you never worked a case before in your life. Alfred Shaw lived someplace, and so did that Wilson fellow. Let's get busy and start asking some questions and noseying around."

Longarm and Matt Carey were standing in the middle of the only uncluttered room they'd found in Alfred Shaw's house. All the other rooms they'd searched through had been in disarray, furniture overturned, the seats of chairs slashed, rugs pulled back, black soot strewn by stoves where the stovepipes had been disassembled.

"I'd imagine we can be sure about two things," Carey said. "Since we didn't find the gold bags in Wilson's place, they'd've had to be here in Shaw's house, and Wilson finally run down the place where Shaw'd kept 'em."

"Likely you're right, but I'd still give a pretty to be sure," Longarm told him. "All we're real sure about is that whether Wilson found the gold or not, it's bound to be what he was looking for. I'd say he had a pretty good idea that Shaw'd stashed it here where it'd be handy if he needed to make a fast getaway. And I'd also say it's more than likely Wilson found the gold."

"Oh, sure," Carey agreed.

"Well, Shaw's dead and Wilson's on the run, so all that's left to do is find him."

"I'm ready to start whenever you are," Carey said quickly.

"Now, Matt, this is your stomping ground," Longarm told him. "But you've got your job all lined up here. You can't go hightailing after Wilson; that's my job. What's your best bet about the way he'd likely be headed?"

"He wouldn't have much of a choice, Longarm. There's too many towns he'd have to dodge through or go around was he to go north or south or to the west, towards the coast. He's bound to've gone east, to the mountains. Likely he'll go straight till he gets to them, because there's a pretty good trail he can turn off on to go south then."

"I figure you're right," Longarm said. "And I don't aim to waste any time taking out after him. But first I need for you to tell me what I'd need to be looking out for."

Carey was silent for a moment, then he said, "Going east into the mountains, a man that's got a heavy load is going to have to take the easiest grades, even if he has got a packhorse. I'd say he'd likely follow the middle fork of the Salmon River till it peters out at Willamette Pass."

"And he'll likely turn south when he gets to the pass?"

"Well, he sure as hell won't go north, because that's a rough upgrade trail. Everybody who knows these parts stays clear of it. Now, the trail south's an old army road that ain't used a lot. It don't go through much settled country but it's not as rough."

"Good," Longarm said. "You got any more ideas that might help me find my way around?"

"I sure wish I did have, Longarm, but I don't."

"What about landmarks?"

"Why, a little ways to the southeast of Crater Butte you'll run into old Fort Klamath. The Indian Bureau used it for a while, tried to turn it into a headquarters for the tribes down that way, but they moved out a year or so ago."

"What about the Indians?" Longarm asked. "Friendly ones, I hope?"

"Oh, sure. The Indians out here never was bad trouble-makers. Why, they don't even fight much among their-selves."

"I reckon you've told me about all I need to know, Matt," Longarm said. "I wouldn't start out on a chase like this if I didn't figure those two bags of double eagles that Wilson fellow's got to be toting are going to slow him down a lot. That oughta be just about the edge I'll need to swing the odds over my way."

"Well, I'd sure like to be riding with you, Longarm. But all this to-do here's going to keep me on the hop."

"All you got to do here is stay a jump ahead of everybody else," Longarm said with a smile. "And I sure ain't going to tell you how to go about that, not in your own jurisdiction. Now I'm going to go scrape me up some grub for my necessary bag and get moving."

Settling back in his saddle as he reined in to survey the long down-slope ahead of him, Longarm finally relighted the cigar he'd allowed to go out almost a half hour ago. During that time he'd been fighting the reins of the livery horse along the trail that bordered the bank of the Salmon River. It had been the most miserably difficult stretch of uphill travel he'd encountered since leaving Grant's Pass.

Longarm had lost count of the number of sheer-walled crevasses that in several places stretched across the trail. The wide earth-cracks had forced him to pick his way around them over stone-hard earth as he sought to find safe footing for his livery mount. There'd also been a half-dozen whitewater tributary creeks to cross. The roiled surface of their rushing water had hidden the streambeds, turning each crossing into a gamble that his horse would retain its footing.

"Old son," Longarm muttered under his breath as he released a wreath of quickly scattered smoke, "the only good thing about this trail is on account of you know that Wilson fellow you're after ain't made much better time than you have. He can't be too far up ahead since he didn't get all that much of a start on you. All you got to do is plug along steady, and you're bound to catch up with him sooner or later."

Glancing at the butt of the cigar he'd taken from his mouth, Longarm pinched off the coal at its tip and dropped the butt to the ground. He toed the horse ahead, letting it pick its way and set its own pace on the winding hoofbeaten stretch of the vestigial trail that stretched in a long down-slope in front of him.

Even in the short distance that separated Longarm from the towering rock formation that rose a short distance ahead, the path wriggled like a worm's trail over baked soil that was more rock than earth before vanishing behind the steep face of the high boulder. Just ahead of the point at which the boulder blocked Longarm's view ahead, the trail seemed to show signs of leveling out.

Longarm turned his head from side to side as he scanned the expanse of rugged country beyond the steep cliff, but he saw nothing moving in the thin stand of struggling pine trees on the boulder-strewn expanse that came into sight below him when he reached the point where the high rock formation rose. Longarm tightened his grip on the reins to slow his mount a bit more as it began balking while it was rounding the trail around the face of the rock formation.

In spite of Longarm's firm grip on its reins, the horse reared up again, and as its forefeet touched the ground it neighed once more. Longarm was forced to cling to the leathers and clamp his legs as tightly as possible around the animal's barrel. He was still tugging the reins, trying to calm the horse down and bring it under control again, and had almost succeeded in stopping the animal's antics, when a man with his face masked by a bandana and holding in his hands a rifle leveled at Longarm stepped from behind the massive rising heap of stone just ahead.

"You just be careful now," the man said. The folded bandana muffled his voice and reduced it to a loud whisper, but did not mask the determination in his speech as he nodded toward the muzzle of his rifle. "Behave right, and I won't have to cut you down. What I want you to do is just set quiet, and not make no moves towards that six-gun of yours, nor your rifle either, because I got a real nervous trigger finger."

To Longarm's surprise, his horse had stopped bucking and stomping the instant the masked man started speaking. Deciding in a flash to obey the highwayman and take his chances at breaking free later, Longarm raised his hands in response to the outlaw's command, but maintained his position in the saddle.

"I don't want to have to kill you," the holdup man went on. "All I want is your money. You just drop your rifle and pull that Colt outa your holster with two fingers and drop it down too. Then you can dig into your pocket and toss down whatever money you got. Soon as I get my hands on the cash, I'll step over to my horse yonder and be on my way."

"Don't look for me to argue with you," Longarm told the highwayman as he opened his hand to let his Colt fall to the ground, then carefully slipped his Winchester from its saddle holster and dropped it beside the Colt. "The little bit of money I got ain't worth getting killed for. You can have it and welcome."

"Once you pass me your cash and I get started moving, you can be on your way," the outlaw said. "I'll have to take your guns, or else you might be tempted to follow me. But just be careful, now, and do like I say."

Holding his arm carefully as far away from his body as possible, Longarm took his wallet from his pocket and tossed it beside the feet of the bandit. He waited until the highwayman squatted to pick it up. Then, as the outlaw glanced down at the wallet, Longarm slid his ace-in-the-hole derringer from its sheath on his forearm, took quick aim, and triggered off his shot.

On the ground the outlaw jerked backward and lay still as the .44-caliber slug from the derringer crashed into his brain. Longarm heaved a long-held sigh of relief and sat motionless in his saddle for another moment or two before giving the bandit's body a thorough inspection.

Chapter 6

Before dismounting, Longarm glanced around quickly to take stock of his surroundings. He was sure that the outlaw who'd challenged him had been alone, for if the dead man had been a member of a gang or working with a partner, his companion or companions would certainly have revealed their presence when the shooting started. Satisfied that he'd not be risking a shot from ambush, he levered out of his saddle.

When his feet hit the ground Longarm picked up his Colt and holstered it. He retrieved the Winchester and slid it into its saddle holster before stepping over to the holdup man's sprawled figure. For a moment or two Longarm stood examining the corpse at close range and paying close attention to the backs of the man's hands. There were no tattoo marks on them.

"Well, old son, that fellow sure wasn't laying for you in particular," he said to himself. "More'n likely he's some poor devil that figured it was easier to turn outlaw than do an honest day's work."

Now Longarm hunkered down beside the body. His quick examination revealed nothing new, and he began the unpleasant task of searching the corpse. His first move was to pick up the outlaw's old Spencer carbine and set it aside; then he pulled away from the dead man's face the bandana which had served him as a mask. The features of the corpse were strange to him, and after he'd studied them for a moment Longarm was sure that he'd have remembered the man's face if he'd ever seen it on a wanted poster.

Now he started a methodical search of the man's pockets. Except for a pair of badly crushed cigars his shirt pockets were empty. One of the side pockets of his trousers held a few cartwheels and some small change. The opposite pocket yielded three cartridges; their caliber was that of the Spencer carbine that had been lying by the corpse.

One hip pocket contained nothing; the other had in it a thin and much-worn leather wallet. Longarm dropped into the bandana the money and cartridges he'd removed from the dead outlaw's body, and gathered its corners into a single bunch in order to make it easier for him to hold while he examined the wallet.

From the billfold's lack of bulk, Longarm had not expected to find a great deal, and his expectation was fulfilled. Aside from three postage stamps and a much-creased tattered-edged sheet of paper, the wallet held only a two-dollar Confederate States banknote and some shreds of tobacco. Unfolding the brittle creases of the piece of paper, he read the few lines of tight script written on it in ink that had faded to a dull and almost indecipherable rusty brown.

There was no date on the page, and the note did not begin with a salutation. It read: "*I got your letter, and I hope it's the last one you'll send me. I don't want to ever see you again, so just keep on going your way and I'll keep going mine.*"

Longarm tried to decipher the scrawled signature on the short letter, but was unable to do so. After a clearly recognizable capital G, the four or five other letters that followed it were nothing more than unrecognizable scribbles.

"It'd sure be a lot easier on a fellow trying to make out what somebody's name is if folks were to write it clear enough so you could read it," Longarm muttered to himself. "Times like this, when you ain't got a single name to work on, a man looking at their scribbles just can't tell who's been doing what or why they did it."

Refolding the fragile sheet of paper, Longarm restored it to the wallet, and added the wallet to the pitifully small yield of other items that he'd collected from the outlaw's pockets. Then he slid the slim packet into one of his saddlebags.

"Well, now, old son," he said into the silent air. "It's certain-sure this fellow had a horse, and likely it ain't too far away. You better make a look-see for it, because in this up-and-down country that livery horse you rented ain't going to hold out long if it's got to carry you and that outlaw's body at the same time."

For a moment or two Longarm surveyed the terrain along the winding downhill trail, looking for a spot where the dead outlaw might have scrabbled up the slanting hillside to the road. His eye-search was rewarded quickly. Fifty or sixty feet from the spot where the holdup man had appeared he could make out several small streaks of freshly disturbed earth on the slope leading to the tiny meadow below.

After he'd stood studying the lines of broken surface soil for a few moments, Longarm was more certain than ever that they could only have been made by booted feet mounting the steep slope. They started at the bottom of the slope, where a crescent of green grass and scrub bushes stretched from the base of the rise to a cluster of trees that rose at the far side of the little clearing.

"Well, old son," Longarm said, his voice sounding strange to him in the still air. "You better have a look-see around down below there. Those trees on that level spot's the only place around here close where that dead fellow could hide a horse, and that nag you're riding sure ain't going to carry double. Besides all that, you ain't got a shovel to dig him a grave, and it just wouldn't be right to leave his body laying here on the trail, even if somebody else'd likely stumble across it before it's had time to rotten out."

Returning to his mount, Longarm pulled its reins free of their saddlehorn loop and let them drop to the ground. He glanced around to choose the heaviest boulder he could manage to lift, picked it up, and lowered it on the ends of the dangling leathers to anchor them.

For a moment he considered carrying his rifle with him. Then, since he'd seen no movement inside the grove of trees near the base of the drop-off, he decided that the rifle would only be a hindrance during his descent to the base, and dismissed the extra precaution as being unnecessary.

Longarm took time to secure the the dead outlaw's Spencer carbine to his saddlestrings before he began to pick his way down the steep slanting side of the incline. He found the first few yards easy going, for the side of the drop-off was a rounded shoulder that had only a gentle slope. Then the shoulder gave way to steeper ground, and though he leaned a bit backward and braced each foot as best he could, the earth grew looser as he descended.

Long before he reached the level ground at the bottom of the slope, Longarm was forced to take short fast strides to save himself from plummeting down to the level stretch at the bottom of the incline. He was moving to the next thing at a dead run when he got to the flat grass-covered surface of the hollow.

For few moments he stood motionless while catching his breath. Then he fished out a cigar and a match. Closing his jaws on the stogie, he flicked his thumbnail across the head of the match and stood motionless, scanning the area.

There was very little to see on the flat terrain stretching away from the base of the rise Longarm had just descended. A wide expanse of knee-high prairie grasses swayed gently in the breeze from the spot where he stood, and a long thick line of ponderosa pines rose perhaps a hundred yards away beyond the crescent-shaped stand of tall wind-rippled grass.

Then, at one point in the wide stretch of trees, Longarm glimpsed a hint of movement. He nodded to himself and started toward the movement as he said, "That'd be the outlaw's horse for sure, old son. So you might as well mosey over to it and see if you can catch it and get it up that grade to the trail. It ain't going to be no easy job, but it's one you got to do."

Pushing his way through the waist-high brush, Longarm started toward the stand of pines. He took no special pre-cautions other than occasionally scanning the terrain around him. He was sure by now that if the dead outlaw had been working with a partner, the second man would certainly have made his presence known at the beginning of the brief spell of gunplay.

Longarm reached the trees and stepped into a long nar-row glade that had been hidden by the trees. Then his jaw dropped, the cigar in his mouth fell to the ground, and he came to a sudden halt while he stared in amazement at the scene that now met his eyes.

Spaced in a line across the stunted growth of low-waving grass in the long clearing the skeletons of a half-dozen horses gleamed whitely. The milky shine of their rib cages and leg bones and their elongated skulls made a sharp con-trast to the narrow expanse of dark earth on which they lay.

The line of skeletons stretched from one end of the glade to the other.

Dark twisted strips of leather bridles and cheek pieces formed thick black lines against the bleached chalk-white skulls and jaws; age-yellowed teeth were visible in the skeletal jawbones. A few sprigs of weeds protruded from the rib cages of the horse skeletons, and at the ends of their bleached leg bones blackened hooves made the leg bones look even whiter than they were.

It was the same contrast produced by that between the ivory-white ribs of the dead horses and almost black hue of the weatherbeaten saddles that were still lying askew at the center of their spines, their girth straps sagging and twisted at the ends of the animals' ribs.

Longarm picked up his fallen cigar and relighted it while he studied the skulls of the animals and the dark strips of harness leather that ran from their skeletal jaws to the long bole of a dead tree to which they had been hitched.

"Old son," he muttered, his subdued voice sounding loud in the silence of the little glade, "what in tarnation could've taken place here?"

Longarm was now studying more closely the details of the scene he'd stumbled onto, running his eyes along the row of horse skeletons. For the first time he noticed a number of splintered and burred patches on the long tree trunk to which the animals had been tethered. He gazed at the splintered areas spaced almost equidistantly along the long tree bole, and then ran his eyes across the prone horse skeletons for several moments.

"Those poor damn horses," Longarm said at last. "They were just left hitched up there till they got so hungry they tried to chew up that tree and eat it. Now, whoever it was left 'em to starve to death that way oughta be . . ."

Breaking off, Longarm stood silently again for a short while, flicking his eyes along the line of horse skeletons. "You got confused for a minute there, old son. The fellows that hitched those horses on that tree trunk weren't just being mean or careless. They didn't come back to tend to 'em because somebody was chasing 'em and the whole bunch must've been killed in a shootout."

He stood for a moment, long enough to puff on his cigar before going on. "Whatever kinda fracas it was that took place here had to be a long time past. Maybe it was soldiers chasing redskins or maybe it was the other way around, or it could've been a bunch of outlaws running for cover with a posse after 'em. Anyway, whatever it was, it happened so long ago that it don't make no never-mind now."

Longarm had released another puff or two of blue-gray smoke and tossed away the stub of his cigar. "Right now you got a job of your own to tend to, catching that dead outlaw's horse and getting on the tracks of that Wilson fellow. You better let whoever comes along this way next puzzle things out. You got business to tend to, and there ain't too much daylight left, so catch that dead fellow's horse you came down after. Best thing you can do is forget you ever saw all these skeletons here and move on down the road to where you're heading."

For what seemed to have been an interminable time Longarm had been circling the base of a high-rising mountain peak on his right and that of an equally high mesa on his left. He'd had a long slow ride, and both the led horse carrying the body of the outlaw he'd been forced to shoot and his own livery mount were showing signs of fatigue.

During the two days that had passed since his brush with the outlaw he'd forged ahead on the narrow winding up-and-down trail from first dawn until after sunset. Now, his own muscles were beginning to twitch a time or two each time he made a sudden move, or one that required unusual exertion.

For the last few miles Longarm had traveled he'd noticed a change in the terrain; it was more down-slope now than up-and-down, and the land stretching away from both sides of the trail had become a series of expanses of yellowing soil broken only by the humps of a few hillocks.

There'd been changes in the narrow path as well. It was a bit wider and instead of being pocked only with hoofprints, there were a few wagon-wheel ruts in the softer stretches. The spreads of baked earth were now less numerous than they'd been earlier, and in the course of the last few miles he'd traveled there had been times he'd had to follow the weaving wheel ruts to avoid mounting small hillocks.

"Well, old son," Longarm mused aloud as he let his horse set its own gait on the narrow winding trail, "about all you can do is hope this is the same way that damn Wilson fellow's been traveling. But it stands to reason it is, because Matt Carey said it's the only way he could miss the big towns where there'd be lawmen to nab him. And the last thing Wilson would want to do is hide those two sacks of gold. He'd be afraid to try hiding 'em, because somebody might stumble onto 'em."

Longarm broke off his soliloquy for he'd reached a fork in the trail. He reined in and bent forward in his saddle, trying to choose between the two narrow strips of well-beaten earth. Either of them could have been the trail which had been taken by Wilson.

None of the hoofprints Longarm was inspecting looked fresh, but he'd gotten accustomed to taking the branch of a road fork that showed greatest number of hoofprints and wagon ruts. Here, the signs finally failed him. There was little difference between the two forks; they each appeared to be used by about the same number of travelers. The wagon-wheel ruts were almost equally deep and the hoofprints were virtually the same for each fork.

"Now, you got a real puzzle here, old son," Longarm said under his breath as he fished a fresh cigar from his pocket. When he'd lighted the long slim cheroot, he went on. "It don't look like either of these trails gets more travelers than the other one. Maybe you should just toss up a cartwheel and call heads or tails, and hope it falls the right way."

Intending to turn his idle thought into reality, Longarm reached into the pocket of his jeans to get a coin. He was still fumbling among the loose change his fingers encountered when a distant drumming of hoofbeats reached his ears. With the prospect of being able to get some accurate directions from the approaching traveler, Longarm settled back into his saddle and waited for the oncoming rider to reach him.

He did not have long to wait. The hoofbeats grew louder, and soon after he'd first heard their thunkings the horse and its rider appeared around the left-hand fork of the trail. Longarm breathed a long-held sigh of relief when he saw that the man on the horse wore a gray shirt and blue pantaloons, the field uniform of the army's cavalry forces. Sitting back in his saddle, Longarm waited for the soldier to reach him.

Obviously the approaching cavalryman had seen Longarm at about the same time that Longarm had gotten a clear look at him. He began checking his horse's gait while there was still a long span of road between them, and reined to a halt when he reached Longarm. When he saw the body on the horse Longarm was leading a frown swept over the soldier's face. Before he spoke he dropped his right hand to the butt of the revolver in its hip holster.

"Well, stranger, you've got a real odd load on that horse you're leading," he said. "Maybe you'd better explain it."

"Be glad to," Longarm replied. "My name's Long, Custis Long, deputy U.S. marshal outa the Denver office."

"You're a long ways from home," the officer said. "But if you're a U.S. marshal, I'd imagine you can dig up a badge to show me and prove it?"

"That won't be a bit of trouble," Longarm replied. "Just don't get upset now and start shooting when I reach back to my hip pocket and get it out to show you."

Moving slowly after the army officer had nodded agreement, Longarm took his wallet from his pocket and flipped it open to give the soldier a look at his badge.

"I've seen marshals' badges before," the officer said. "And yours looks real enough, Marshal Long. Now that we know what's what, my name's Rogers, Lieutenant Frank Rogers. Stationed at Fort Klamath—it's back a ways past a fork in the road. And I'd guess that body you've got draped across the led horse is an outlaw of some kind?"

"You guessed right, Lieutenant," Longarm told him. "He tried to hold me up a good ways back, and I had to shoot him. I didn't feel like I could just leave him laying across the road, but the ground was too hard for me to dig him a grave, even if I had a shovel, which I don't. I reckon you can see I didn't have much choice but to bring him along. I figure to hand him over to the first marshal's office I come to up ahead."

"Well, there's a cemetery back at the fort," the soldier said. "I guess you could give him to the chaplain to bury, since we're both working for Uncle Sam."

"Now, I'll just take you up on that," Longarm said. "And I don't imagine I need to tell you I'm right glad to meet up with you. Maybe you could tell me a thing or two that'd get me on the track of the outlaw I'm after."

"We don't have much truck with outlaws at Fort Klamath," Rogers replied. "Or with anybody from your outfit either. But go ahead and trot out your question. I'll try to answer it."

"I'm after a crook that's trying to get away with some sacks of gold coins he stole, but I lost his trail quite a ways back. All I know for sure is he was headed in this direction."

"An outlaw carrying sacks of gold coins?" Rogers asked. "Money that he stole, I suppose?"

"Oh, he stole it, all right. Killed the head man of the gang he was tied up with, and took off with the gold."

"And you've tracked him to this part of the country?"

"Well, I been chasing after this thief for quite a spell," Longarm replied. "He ain't the first crook I've had to run down. But the best I can tell you is that the one I'm after now is likely headed this way, if he ain't already passed your fort."

Rogers looked startled.

Chapter 7

Longarm noticed the lieutenant's reaction. "Does that mean you might have seen him?" he asked. Rogers shook his head. "That's something I can't be sure about. But we don't get a lot of visitors at Fort Klamath. I guess it's because the road we're on goes through that big Indian reservation to the south of it and doesn't lead to much of anyplace to the north."

"Well, now, from what I've heard, there was a bunch of forts that were just sorta scattered out around here, back in the days when the redskins were pretty wild," Longarm said.

"I've heard the same thing," Rogers said. "And Fort Klamath is certainly one of those scattered forts. I understand that it was set up after all the wagon trains started pushing this way. We still have a few emigrant wagons stop, mostly to buy victuals, but today the railroads carry most emigrant families."

"And there's not any railroad lines close by?"

"Not unless almost a hundred miles is what you call close. And with the Indians all peaceful now, there's been some latrine talk lately that the fort's likely to be closed before long."

"You mean the redskins don't bother you anymore?"

"Not exactly that, Marshal. We still get some dustups, but most of the Indians hereabouts aren't from the warlike tribes. And there's a big Indian Agency office on down to the south a little ways. They take care of most of the trouble that comes along. The hardcase Indians are what we deal with at the fort, them and the ones that come to buy grub or trade their geegaws for it at our commissary."

"You'd have a pretty good-sized one, I'd imagine, set away from any towns like you are," Longarm said.

"Fair to middling," Rogers agreed. "I understand this used to be a busy place, but the Indians are about the only visitors we have. Maybe some emigrant wagons stop, like I said, but not much else."

"Well, Lieutenant, it ain't redskins or emigrants I'm looking for," Longarm said. "The fellow I'm after might call himself Wilson, but he's just as likely to be passing under another name. To save you asking, he's big and sorta mean-looking. He's traveling with his own horse and a led horse that's carrying some real heavy saddlebags. Oh, yes, this fellow's got one mark you'd be likely to notice if you get a good close-up look at him. He's got a funny-looking scar on the back of his right hand."

"Well, the only white man who's stopped there lately would certainly fit your description, Marshal Long. He stopped by two days ago. He was big and looked like he had a grudge against everybody in the world. I didn't pay a lot of attention to him, but I did notice he had a puckered place—I'd guess it to be a scar—on the back of one of his hands."

"That scar you saw on his hand, did it maybe look something like a fishhook?"

Rogers thought for a moment, then said slowly, "Now that you mentioned it, I'd say it did. I couldn't help getting a real good look at both of his hands—he was busy pointing at what he wanted to buy in the commissary—and I think the scar was on his right hand."

"Then it's just about sure he's likely to be the scoundrel I'm after," Longarm concluded. "I hope you noticed what sorta rig he was traveling with?"

"If I did, I don't remember . . ." Lieutenant Rogers broke off and the ghost of a frown flitted across his face. "Now, wait a minute. Maybe I do remember something. The day I saw that fellow, when I was going to the commissary from my quarters, I recall seeing two strange horses at the commissary hitch rail. I didn't see an army brand on either one, so I looked at them a bit closer than I would have otherwise. One was a saddle horse, the other one was a packhorse. I can't tell you much else, but the saddle horse was roan. The packhorse was a dun, and as I recall it had a pretty good load on it."

"Well, that's just the kinda help I been needing," Longarm told the soldier. "Now, before I get on my way again, would you have any ideas about where this outlaw we're talking about might've taken off for?"

"From the questions I heard him asking I got the idea he was headed west," Rogers replied. "I remember he asked the quartermaster about the trails he'd need to take to get to Medford, but that's about all that stuck in my mind."

"That sounds pretty much like I figured," Longarm said thoughtfully. "Now, if what I've been told is right, Medford'd be a pretty good stretch to the west from here."

"It is," the lieutenant agreed.

"That just might be enough to give me the lead I been needing," Longarm said. "Now, I'll just keep on going till I catch up with him."

"Marshal Long, I don't want to be responsible for setting you out on what might turn into a wild-goose chase," the officer said. "Why don't you ride on with me back to the fort and talk to Sergeant Larson? He's in charge of the commissary, and I'm sure he could be a lot more help to you than I can. Besides that, we've got some field maps there that might help you."

Longarm was silent for a moment. "How much of a ride is it from here to your fort?"

"Six, maybe seven miles, but it's an easy ride. And you can get that dead outlaw on the led horse buried at the fort."

Longarm shook his head. "I thank you for the invite, Lieutenant, but I don't reckon I better take it. Right now this fellow I'm after has got a two-day start on me, so I'm going to have to do some catching up. But I'd be much obliged if you could take this body off my hands."

"Certainly, Marshal. As I said, I'm sure the chaplain will do the honors. I hope the other fellow is the one you're after, and I hope you catch him," Rogers said. "I guess you know the country hereabouts?"

"Not as good as I'd like to," Longarm admitted. "I'd take it real kindly if you got any tips you can give me on how the land lays to the west of here."

"At this time of the afternoon you can just ride right into the sun," the lieutenant replied. "You'll have three or four small rivers and a pretty fair number of good-sized creeks to ford, but none of them's all that bad to get across. You'll know the Rogue River by its size when you get to it, and the country along it is pretty well settled up by now."

"If that's the case, there'll likely be a few ranches or maybe some farms where this outlaw might've stopped, or where there might be somebody who's seen him," Longarm said thoughtfully.

"Well. I've heard from some of the fellows who were stationed further west that there was a rush of settlers there a few years ago. That'd be in the country I'd imagine this fellow you're after is heading for."

"Well, I'll run him down sooner or later, and the quicker I get started looking, the better. So I'll just thank you for your help, and be on my way."

Exchanging good-bye waves with the army officer, Longarm reined his horse around and started riding, his face into the sun. As he pushed on, the occasional stands of pine trees were spaced further and further apart on the broken rocky soil and the trail became fainter and fainter.

Now and then Longarm passed a stretch of stump-covered ground where three or four sagging unpainted cabins stood. He could tell at a glance that all of them were the remains of long-abandoned clear-cut timber stands. Longarm stopped at the first three groups of cabins that he encountered, and at each one he made a quick examination of the deteriorating structures, looking for signs that someone had sheltered in them recently.

In the third group he found clear evidence that it had been used within the past few days. In front of one of the cabins there were mounds of horse dung, not yet dried to the crumbling stage. Inside, there were both ashes and coals in the little mud-plastered stone fireplace, and while the winds had swept the hearths of the other cabins clean of ashes, in this one there was fresh flaky ash as well as small coal chunks from a fire that had been kindled in it recently.

"A-course, it might not've been that Wilson fellow who left these coals and ashes," Longarm mused aloud. "But whoever it was that stopped here, they couldn't be more than a day or two ride up ahead right now."

Encouraged by his discovery, Longarm continued pulling off the road and stopping at each of the abandoned cabins he encountered. Although there was no evidence of recent fires in the next several cabins, and although the trail itself gave no positive indication that Wilson had passed that way, Longarm continued checking the cabins and the riverbanks and their streambeds.

Mostly he confined his examinations of the cabins to a quick look around, just long enough to be sure that he was missing no details of their interiors. He found only one other that showed signs of recent occupancy, though the evidence he looked at yielded no fresh clues.

But the signs that Longarm noted on the banks and bottoms of the streambeds gave him an occasional signal that his quarry was still ahead of him. At the water's edge he looked for and more often than not found the crescent-shaped tracks of recently made hoofprints.

In the wider creeks where the currents were lightest, Longarm's harvest of clues was the greatest. In a few, where the stream was wide and shallow and its flow was slow, the prints of horses' hooves remained almost undisturbed by the gentler currents that ran close to the stream banks. Always he looked for the impressions of the hooves of two horses, one set of prints shallow, the second set deep, left by a horse that was carrying a heavier load than a rider.

But stopping and examining each of the abandoned logging camps as well as the bed of every stream he crossed took its toll of time and energy. After he'd been on the move for four days, Longarm found himself becoming bone-weary long before the onset of darkness compelled him to begin looking for a place to camp.

Before he'd crossed too many creeks he saw a small stand of trees ahead and the fading shine of rippling water in one of the creeks that disappeared into the grove. Reaching the trees, Longarm reined his horse off the road and into the widely spaced trees.

"Well, old son," he said into the growing dimness as he reined in at the beginning of a small open space. "This looks like as good a place as any other one you'd find was you to push on. And there ain't no use in traveling further now it's getting so dark. You might just as well stop right here."

After tethering his horse near a small grassed knoll where it could graze, Longarm unsaddled it and spread his saddle pad, then tossed his blanket roll on it before dragging his saddlebags within easy reach. Hunkering down on the rolled blankets, he made a quick meal from the scant rations the bags contained.

After his hunger had been satisfied, Longarm lighted a cigar and puffed it while finishing his cursory preparations for the night. The simple jobs of unrolling the blankets and placing his rifle on the edge of the makeshift bed completed, he double-folded his saddle pad for a pillow, laid his Colt beside it, and stretched out on his makeshift bed. Within two minutes after he'd snuffed out the butt of his cigar, he was asleep.

"Damned if this Klamath country ain't tricky," Longarm muttered to himself as he stood up in his stirrups and looked at the rushing water, its surface almost hidden by a covering of roiling froth. "You sure didn't figure on having to swim a horse across this big of a river."

In both directions, upstream and down from the spot where he'd reined in, the blue-gray surface of the wide stream bubbled and splashed as far as he could see. The rays of the bright early morning sun glinting on the stream were reflected in such a constantly changing fashion from the frothy bubbles that Longarm's straining eyes could make out nothing below the river's rippled surface.

As he squinted along the roiling water, Longarm saw a dozen spots strung out in both directions where the bubbles gave way to shining stretches that were free of the froth. However, these clear surface patches glistened so brightly that they were as impenetrable as the remainder of the stream.

"Now, maybe this is the Rogue River, old son," Longarm said to himself. "And even if the trail stops here, it picks up on the other side. So what you better do is put the little pot in the big pot and let your horse find its own way across."

His decision made, Longarm slacked the reins he'd been holding taut and prodded the horse's flank with the toe of his boot. The animal hesitated only a moment before entering the stream. Then it moved ahead, ignoring the rush of the knee-deep current. It lowered its forelegs slowly, scuffing them on the riverbed for a moment now and then before advancing carefully. In a few places it moved ahead unhesitatingly; in others its progress was slow and careful. Several times, when the horse seemed over-anxious to move, Longarm was tempted to tug on the reins, but resisted the temptation almost as soon as it struck him.

Though it seemed a long time to Longarm, the crossing was completed successfully in a few minutes. The horse mounted the opposite bank with Longarm's boots still dry and only the animal's haunches dripping. At the top of the gently slanting bank, Longarm reined in and looked back over his shoulder at the stream.

"All right, now, you've made it across another stream, old son," he said aloud as he bent in the saddle to look at the half-dozen sets of hoofprints in the soft soil of the trail.

At this stage of his long chase, Longarm was familiar enough with the double set of hoofprints he was following to recognize them at a glance. He soon found them again, which meant his quarry was still moving ahead of him.

Though the character of the trail had changed little, after he'd crossed the crest of the low ridge and started moving down its winding sinuous curves, the land itself was no longer the same. There were no more thick stands of timber, but many more forests of stumps. The grades were easier, and on the level expanse that started at the end of the down-slope ahead he could see a checkerboard pattern of fences and the blocky forms of houses and barns.

Longarm continued to talk aloud as he let his horse set its own gait on the long down-slope. "Well, old son," he said, "now that you're on the other side of 'em, you got to admit getting over those hills wasn't nowhere near as bad a job as it looked. Now all you got to do is keep going and move along steady until you catch up with that Wilson fellow."

Daylight was beginning to wane, and Longarm was thinking of finding a place to stop for the night, when he reached the sprawl of farmhouses that had seemed so close when seen from the crest of the high ridge. He'd already started to scan the land ahead, looking on both sides of the road for a place to bed down for the night. When he'd seen the first of the farmhouses, even from a distance he'd known that it had been abandoned.

At close range the small blocky dwelling revealed that its windows had been covered by boards nailed across them. The land around the little dwelling did not support a growing crop, but in its fields a jumble of volunteer shoots mingled with a small forest of weeds. After circling the house on horseback, Longarm did not bother to dismount. He reined the horse back to the two-rut road and started along it again despite the fading daylight.

By the time Longarm had covered half the distance to the next house, the dark night-blue of the cloudless sky was creeping steadily higher on the eastern horizon. There was still enough daylight left for Longarm to study the terrain ahead and the small dwelling that stood just off the wheel-rutted road. The land stretching away from the house showed the same signs of mixed growth that he'd noticed during his inspection of the previous farm.

While he was riding past a field that lay between him and the house Longarm noticed that it showed signs of past cultivation, but that at the present time its growth was what he recognized as volunteer wheat. Most of the plant stalks were already spindly and many of them had broken, their tips slanting to the ground. The field next to it had been planted with apple-tree saplings. Almost all the young trees had fruitless branches and yellowed leaves, and more than a few of them leaned askew, ready to topple over.

Beyond the area of neglected cultivation, the house showed no signs that it was presently being lived in. It was a small house that had probably once been painted a light yellow, though the straggles of peeling paint on its wall made it difficult to be sure what color the paint had been. A rock chimney rose along the rear end-wall to its roof-peak, and a pair of uncurtained windows broke the side wall that was visible to Longarm.

While he'd been passing the field of dead and dying apple-tree saplings and studying the dwelling he was approaching, Longarm had reined off the road, turning his horse toward the house. Now, after examining it at closer range, he decided that the dwelling must be abandoned also, like the farmhouse he'd seen earlier. He changed his mind about making a closer investigation and tugged his reins to turn the horse back to the trail.

Longarm reined his horse toward the corner of the house, paying no attention to the deteriorating dwelling. The trail was only a short distance away, and Longarm was examining the sky to judge how much daylight remained. He passed between the corner of the house and the road, riding at a slant that brought him within a yard or two of the ramshackle little dwelling. His attention was now concentrated on getting back on the trail. He was studying the easiest way to do that when the door of the house burst open and a woman ran onto its narrow porch.

"Wait, mister!" she called. "Don't just ride on past like you're doing! I've been here all by myself for such a long time now that I need somebody I can talk to! Besides, it's getting too late for anybody that don't know that road to keep on it after dark!"

Longarm had reined in before the woman stopped speaking. He shifted in his saddle and stared at her for a moment before asking, "You mean you're out here in the big middle of no place all by yourself?"

"Well, if that's the way it looks to you, that's the way it is. And I don't mind telling you, I get real lonesome sometimes. This happens to be one of them times, and I'd be real grateful to you if you'd just stop and spend the night with me."

Chapter 8

For a moment Longarm could only stare at the young woman on the narrow porch. Then he said, "I ain't certain-sure that I heard you right, ma'am. And I sure don't aim to get my hand caught in a paste-pot by imagining I heard something that you really weren't aiming to say."

"Oh I meant exactly what I said," she told him. "And I hope you won't waste time worrying about me being crazy or running a whorehouse or anything like that."

"That's not at all what I had in mind," Longarm assured her.

"Of course not. But I don't have to do any guessing about you being old enough to know that a man and a woman in bed together do something besides sleeping."

"I hope you don't take offense, ma'am," Longarm went on, "but I'd say you sure ain't making no bones about why you want me to stop here."

"I have very good reasons, but telling you the rest can wait." She stopped short and shook her head. "My name's Rose Danton, if you're curious."

"Now, I got to make you an apology because I didn't

introduce myself proper," Longarm said.

He was still taking stock of the woman as he spoke. There was nothing extraordinary about her features; she was neither ugly nor pretty. Below a pulled-back sweep of reddish hair her high forehead swept down to the arches of eyebrows a bit lighter in hue than her hair. Her eyes were greenish, her cheekbones high, her nose aquiline, her lips full, and her jaw firm.

She had on a gray lindsey-woolsey dress, with a high neckline. The somber-hued garment hung straight from the bulge of her generous breasts almost to the tops of her high-buttoned shoes and effectively hid her body. The shoes were the kind that field-workers favored, almost knee-high with low heels.

Longarm went on. "I'm a deputy United States marshal, Miz Danton, out—"

She broke in. "Please, just call me Rose. I let my tongue slip when I said my name's Danton. It used to be, but after my husband left me I've decided to go back to my maiden name, which is Smith."

"Whatever you say, Miz Smith—Rose, I meant to say. Now, ma'am, I'm out here on a case. Custis Long's the name that's on my badge, but folks generally call me Longarm."

"And which would you rather I call you, Marshal Long?"

"Why, it don't make no never-mind, Rose. You just suit yourself, I answer to all of 'em. And I'm real glad to meet up with you."

"Not as glad as I was when I saw you rein up here instead of just riding on by. But it's getting dark fast, so suppose you take care of your horse. You'd better tether it around in back, in case some sticky-handed horse-thief comes by and tries to steal it."

"Don't worry none about that. I sleep with one ear open," Longarm assured her. "So I'll just do my little chores and come on around to your door when I've finished."

"Good," she said. "And by the way, if you've got any food in your saddlebags, I might be able to serve up a little bit tastier supper than you'll get otherwise."

"There ain't such a much in my saddlebags," Longarm told her. "All I carry is a dabble of trail rations, jerky and hard biscuits, but you're sure welcome to whatever I've got."

Rose smiled a bit wanly. "I'm afraid your trail rations wouldn't add a lot to our supper. Don't worry, Longarm, I've still got enough food on hand for some kind of a meal."

"Now, I ain't aiming to put you to a lot of trouble trying to feed me," Longarm said.

Rose stopped him with a wave of her hand. "It's not a bit of trouble. What I've got's leftovers, so it won't take me but a minute," she said. "Suppose I go fix our supper while you look after your horse. If you've been in the saddle very long I'd imagine you're hungry."

"I ain't about to say I'm starving, but some grub'd sure go down good right about now," Longarm told her. "So you take care of what you've got to do, and I'll be back in a minute or two."

Longarm led his horse around to the back of the house where it would not be seen from the trail. He dismounted, then made short work unsaddling the animal. Wild grass was growing high around the bottom of the house, and he left enough length in the animal's tether to let it graze freely.

Carrying his saddle gear in one hand and his rifle in the other, he returned to the front of the little house. The door was half-open and he stepped inside. He stood motionless for a moment, letting his eyes adjust to the dimness of the early evening dusk, then deposited his rifle and saddle gear against the wall. As he turned around he stood motionless for a moment, taking quick stock of the room he'd entered.

As nearly as Longarm could tell, the big room took up three quarters of the house. A fieldstone hearth rose in the center of the wall to his left, and a mattress covered with tousled bedding lay in one corner beyond the hearth. In the room's center there was a large easy chair; it stood askew, one of its front legs missing. A table occupied the opposite corner; it held two forks, two spoons, a pair of coffee cups, and the stub of a candle in a cracked and chipped saucer.

Two doors stood ajar in the rear wall. Through one of them he could see nothing except an expanse of bare floor in the room beyond it. The other door was open widely enough for him to glimpse the edge of a small cookstove and Rose moving around in front of it.

Before Longarm could start for the kitchen, Rose came in. She carried a large bowl in one hand and two smaller bowls in the other. Stopping beside the table, she deposited the bowls on it and turned to look at Longarm.

"This is the best I can do right now," she said. "Boiled potatoes and the knuckle pieces of my last ham-butt."

"That strikes me just fine," Longarm assured her. "And if it ain't enough, we can dig into what I got left of my trail rations. Or do you figure we better save them so we can have a bite of breakfast tomorrow morning?"

"I'll vote to save them for breakfast," Rose replied promptly. "But we can always change our minds if we're still hungry when we finish what I've got here. We can just use these spoons that're already on the table, and if you're as hungry as I am, it's time right now to sit down and start."

"Now, that sounds like a good idea to me," Longarm said as he stepped up to the table. Rose was already sitting down, and he lowered himself in the chair across the table from her. He went on. "Maybe while we're having supper you'll tell me how you come to be out here all by yourself, such a long ways from no place."

"After we eat," she promised. "And it's not much of a story. Right now, we'd better get on with supper. It's already almost dark inside here, so if you've got a match to spare, you can light the candle."

Longarm took out a match and flicked his thumbnail across its head. The flare of the match seemed very bright in the gathering dusk, and when he lighted the candle-stub its glow was barely bright enough to dispel the gloom of the room. Then he and Rose ate steadily in silence until both their plates were clear. Then Rose stood up and gestured toward the mattress.

"These chairs are just too straight-backed to sit in comfortably," she said. "So suppose we just settle down on the mattress."

"If that suits you, it suits me," Longarm said. "You go on and get comfortable. Soon as I take off my gunbelt and get a cigar going I'll hunker down by you."

Longarm was lighting one of his long slim cigars as he spoke. While he was puffing the stogie until it was drawing easily, he watched Rose move to the mattress and sit down on its edge. Then he stepped up to the opposite end and unbuckled his gunbelt, dropping the belt with its holstered Colt at the edge of the mattress as he lowered himself to it across from her. Crossing his feet Indian-style, he looked at her inquiringly.

"You're ready for me to start my story?" she asked.

"Whenever the spirit moves you," Longarm replied. "But maybe you better get out another candle and I'll set it up on the table, because that one ain't going to last any too long."

"When it burns out, we'll just have to talk in the dark then," she told him. "Because that's the last candle I've got."

"Well, dark's as good as light for talking in," Longarm observed. "Now, I want to hear whatever you feel like telling me, but if you don't mind listening to some of the things I got strung together, why don't I just tell you about 'em first? You can stop me if I get too far off of the track."

Rose did not reply for a moment; then she nodded and said, "Go ahead, Longarm. I'm sort of curious now to see what you've figured out."

"Well, for openers, you and your husband got a halfway notion that you'd do better out here in this new Oregon country than you would at home, wherever that was, back East," he said. "First thing you knew, your feet got to itching and you made up your minds to move here, because you were certain-sure you could stake out a homestead claim and have more land than you could ever hope to buy back East."

While Longarm was talking the coal of his cigar had faded and died. He took out a match and flicked it into flame with his thumbnail. He was puffing the cigar stub to life again when Rose spoke.

"I can see that you know about us," she said. "Is that because of the farms you saw coming here where people just like us staked land claims?"

"Oregon ain't the only place where folks have staked out land claims, Rose," he replied. "And my job's taken me to a lot of 'em. Sure, I figured it out. It wasn't all that hard."

"Then I expect you know the rest of it before I even start telling you about what happened," she said.

"Pretty much. But even if I might guess real close to what else there is to it, suppose you go ahead and cross the t's and dot the i's," Longarm told her.

After a moment of silence, Rose began. "It was fine when we first got out here. Brad—my husband—worked hard. I helped him as best I could, building this little house and clearing brush-stands off our land. He planted wheat and rode all the way up to Eugene to get the fruit trees to set out."

Rose broke off her narration and Longarm said, "So the two of you made out pretty good until this year, or maybe last year. But while I was riding up to your place, I didn't need to look real hard to see you ain't doing good right now. Did I hit the mark, or am I wrong?"

"You're right, of course," Rose replied, "This year— well, I'm sure you saw how everything dried up because there wasn't enough rain when we really needed it."

"I figured that up," Longarm said. "And if it makes you feel bad to talk about it, I reckon I can guess the rest."

"No," she said firmly. "The only way I can get what's happened out of my mind is to talk about it. It's not that I enjoy . . ." She broke off as the candle flame wavered and went out.

"Don't bother about the candle," Longarm said. "Just go right on. The fire'll give us enough light to see by, and I ain't tired of listening."

Rose was silent for another moment, then went on. "There's not much more to tell. Brad turned mean, hateful-mean. He wouldn't listen to me or talk to me much. It wasn't long before he started going in to Butte Falls—that's the closest little town to here—and staying a day or two."

"You mean he left you by yourself, and just went into town for no reason at all?"

"Sometimes he'd tell me he had to buy something, but if he did, I never saw it when he got back," Rose replied. "But that didn't go on very long. We ran out of money and he began carrying our furniture into town and selling it. We had a rickety little old wagon we found on a claim somebody'd left. He'd fixed it up so we could use it. Then . . ."

When Rose's voice faltered and she said nothing more, Longarm told her, "Now, hashing over the bad things that happened won't help you a bit, Rose. When I first saw you and you said your husband had left you, I sorta figured there'd been some kind of bust-up."

"We didn't really have what you'd call a bust-up," she said. "It's been almost a month since Brad left. He just got up one morning and rode off in the wagon with another piece of furniture. He didn't even wake me up to say good-bye or leave me a letter or anything else. I don't know where he went or where he is now. I don't think I even want to know."

"Well, that might be the best thing that happened for both of you," Longarm suggested. "Now he's gone, so you can go back to wherever you call home. You'll likely forget about him and be able to start all over again."

Rose shook her head. "Not if you mean that I'd get married again," she said. "I'd be afraid that I'd get another man like Brad. Besides, I've already decided what I want to do. I'm going to Butte Falls and be a saloon girl."

Longarm was too surprised to say anything for a moment. Then he said, "I guess you've got it all figured out?"

"Yes. At least, I think I have. Sometimes when I went with Brad to Butte Falls to do our trading, I used to sit in the wagon outside the saloon while he went in to have a drink or two and buy a bottle of whiskey to bring home."

"And I don't reckon that tickled your fancy much?"

"I certainly didn't begrudge Brad a drink or two, but most always I'd get a look inside the saloon when somebody pushed the swinging doors open. Then I'd see the girls up at the bar, wearing their fancy outfits and cuddling up to Brad and the other men, and—well, after he'd left me here by myself I just decided that if they could do it, I could too."

"Now, I reckon I've put in my share of time in saloons here and there, Rose," Longarm said. "And some of the girls I've met up within 'em are happy as jaybirds to be doing what they are, and some don't like it any too much."

"If I don't like being a saloon girl, I can always quit. But if I do, I . . ." Rose broke off and sat silently for a moment before saying, "I'm sure you've been with saloon girls, Longarm. Maybe you can tell me how I'd do if I was one of them."

"Well, now, it ain't my way to say no to a lady when she asks me," Longarm said, "And I sure—"

Before Longarm could finish speaking, Rose had levered herself across the mattress. She stopped and kneeled in front of Longarm, her arms going around him as she sought his lips. He felt her questing tongue and parted his lips to let her thrust it in, then met it with his own.

While they held their tongue-probing kiss the moments ticked off, Rose clinging to Longarm as he slid his arm around her. After a moment she freed one arm, holding him pressed to her with the other while slipping her free hand down to his crotch. Longarm twisted around a bit to make her explorations easier.

As soon as Rose realized the reason for his slight twisting movement she brought her hand up to his belt. She had a bit of difficulty with its buckle before she had it open.

Then she started running her hands over Longarm, and then began to free the buttons of his shirt. Before she'd reached his waist, Longarm leaned back and flicked his fingers quickly along his fly, unbuttoning it. Rose's hands were dropping to Longarm's waist before he'd finished. She brushed his hands aside to push down the waistband of his trousers, and freed his erection while Longarm was levering out of his boots.

When Rose began caressing Longarm, he slid the broad neck of her blouse off her shoulders to bare her breasts. Bending forward, he started kissing them and rasping his tongue over their pebbled tips. After a moment or two, Rose's body started to wriggle and shiver, and as she felt Longarm's erection growing firmer she began writhing and jerking her hips.

Suddenly she twisted her body away from him and rose to her knees as she said, "We're as ready now as we'll ever be, so let's quit acting like we're children."

"That sure suits me," he replied. "It ain't that I'm not enjoying your feel of me, but feeling just ain't enough."

Rose shrugged out of her dress as Longarm dropped his jeans to the floor and stepped away from them before stripping off his shirt and long underwear. Rose had freed herself of the dress and was kneeling on the mattress watching Longarm. She gasped when she saw him jutting and dropped back on the mattress, spreading her thighs in invitation. Longarm kneeled in front of her, and as he bent forward Rose placed the tip of his firm erection.

Then Longarm drove and Rose loosed a small gasp as he went into her. She squirmed and brought up her hips to meet his lunge, rearing on the mattress as she clasped her legs around his hips. She moaned with delight as he found his rhythm, and each time that he thrust she locked her legs around his hips to pull him deeper.

As Longarm continued to drive in a steady slow-paced rhythm, Rose moaned when he started each deep stroke, and cried out with delight as each strong lunge ended. When Longarm felt her body beginning to ripple, he thrust deeply and held himself buried until Rose's quivering faded. Then he resumed his stroking, slowly at first, but increasing the tempo bit by bit until Rose's rhythm of lifting her hips to meet him faltered and broke.

Longarm stopped thrusting then. He held himself pressed to Rose's quivering body, buried deeply. Rose lay quiet for a few moments, while her small shudders faded. When she tried to raise her hips again, Longarm pressed more firmly than ever, holding her still.

"What's wrong?" Rose whispered.

"Not a thing," he replied. "Except it ain't time for us to quit yet."

When Rose did not reply, Longarm began thrusting slowly once more, slow deliberate drives that soon brought back the shivers that had been shaking her before he stopped. Rose met his lusty thrusts, and soon the small murmurs began forming in her throat again. As Longarm increased the tempo of his drives the murmurs grew in volume and in tempo.

This time, Longarm did not slow his thrusts or space them out. He speeded his drives closer together, and lunged as deeply as before. Rose responded almost at once. The quivering that had almost vanished from her body returned in a rush. Suddenly she began gasping, great lusty throaty cries.

Longarm did not break his quickened pace. He was nearing his own climax now, and read Rose's responding jerking heaves. He felt her body begin vibrating at a tempo it had not shown before, and knew that his own time of restraint was growing short.

When Rose's hips started to twist unceasingly and the volume of the small screams bursting from her lips grew louder and sharper, Longarm speeded his strokes. He was driving now in deep lusty thrusts. Rose's cries rose to a quivering peak, and Longarm felt himself beginning to shudder at a tempo which matched hers.

Now he lunged with a deep final thrust as he began jetting. He held himself firmly against Rose's quivering form while she tossed and her cries peaked and then slowly began to subside. At last a final quiver swept her palpitating form and she no longer tried to bring up her hips. Then the spasm of finality swept Longarm. He relaxed in a series of small shudders and lay as supine as Rose was until his quivering ended.

After a moment Rose whispered, "I like to feel you on me and in me. Can't we just stay together this way while we have a little nap?"

"Why, sure, if that's what you want to do. I feel like I could nap a bit myself."

"Good," she sighed. "Just remember I'm a light sleeper. All you'll have to do wake me up is touch me with your fingertip. I'll be awake the minute you do, and we'll . . ." Her voice trailed away as slumber took hers.

"Don't worry, I won't forget," Longarm replied. He did not move except to squirm enough to drop his head on the pillow where Rose's head rested. In a moment he too was sleeping soundly.

Chapter 9

"You're sure you want to go in there by yourself and ask for that job you made up your mind to get?" Longarm asked Rose.

They were standing in front of the saloon in Butte Falls, the early afternoon sun beating down on them.

"You know I'm not going to change my mind about what I've been planning to do, Longarm," Rose replied. "And I know you've got to get back to your own job, so I think the best thing for us to do is to say our good-byes right now."

"Well, I can't argue about that," Longarm told her. "But it ain't going to make me feel good to go on and leave you here."

"I'm a long way past the schoolgirl stage," Rose said with a smile. "I appreciate your thoughtfulness, but I've learned to look out for myself. After last night, though, I'd like nothing better than to spend a lot more nights with you, even if both of us realize it's impossible."

"Sure," Longarm said. "We both got sense enough to know that. You got your troubles and I got mine, which is to find out if I'm still on the track of that crook I'm after. I need to move fast as I can. It's real likely he passed through here, maybe even stopped, so I'm aiming to ask some questions and find out. Now, if you change your mind—"

"I won't," Rose broke in quickly, her voice firm.

"Then about all I can say is, good luck and take care of yourself," Longarm told her.

"Good-bye then, Longarm," Rose said.

She did not wait for him to reply, but turned at once and started across the small strip of ground between them and the saloon. Longarm waited long enough to watch her reach the building and push through the swinging doors, then turned away and led his horse at an angle across the rutted dusty street. He headed for the building which he'd noticed as he and Rose rode into town. It bore a sign, "Blacksmith & Livery & Hardware."

As he drew closer to his objective, Longarm could hear the ringing of a hammer pounding metal on an anvil. He looped the reins of his horse around the hitch rail in front of the building and stepped inside. Just as he stopped in the open doorway to glance around the interior the clanging noises ended.

Longarm saw the blacksmith dropping his hammer to the dirt floor, but before he could call to the man the smith turned away from the anvil, lifting tongs which held a length of strap-iron. The metal was still dull red at one end, but the color was fading rapidly. Longarm waited to speak until the workman had thrust the length of metal into the coals of his forge and turned to start back to the anvil.

"Something I can do for you, stranger?" the blacksmith asked when he saw Longarm.

"I sure hope there is," Longarm replied. "But it ain't blacksmithing work I'm after, it's information. My name's

Long, Custis Long. I'm a deputy United States marshal, and I'll be glad to show you my badge if you'd like to take a look at it."

"I might ask you to do that if you hadn't offered," the smith said. "But since you did, I'll take your word for it. My name's Sam Ellis. Suppose you go ahead and tell me what's got a federal marshal coming here to Butte Falls."

"Why, there ain't no secret about it," Longarm replied. "I'm chasing after a fellow that likely passed through here a day or so back."

"Crook or outlaw of some kind, I reckon?" Ellis asked. "You being a U.S. marshal."

"Oh, sure," Longarm, replied. "And the reason I'm after him is because he stole a big lot of government gold. I'm right sure he's got two horses, the one he'll be riding and a packhorse that's toting a right heavy load. He'd likely have passed this way two or three days ago, but I don't figure I'm much more'n that to catching up with him."

"Then I reckon you know he's someplace up ahead of you?" the blacksmith asked.

"Well, he's left a pretty clear trail so far, which means I need to keep after him before it gets too cold," Longarm replied. "I'd imagine you'd know the same way I do that a man on the run has got to take good care of his horses, so I figured he might've stopped here."

"Well, I always like to help the law," the blacksmith replied. "And there ain't much I miss about what's going on hereabouts, so if you'll tell me a little bit about this man you're after, I'll do the best I can to give you a hand."

"I sorta figured you would," Longarm said. "The crook I'm trying to chase down is a big fellow, and like I said, he'd be traveling with a led horse that's got a right heavy load. Two sacks of stolen gold. Even if I ain't certain-sure he's passed through here, I do know he was headed this way last time I crossed his trail."

"Big fellow, you say?" The smith frowned. "Riding a roan and leading a dun?"

"That's about right. And his led horse oughta have looked like it was plumb tuckered," Longarm added. "I figured if anybody'd seen him, it might've been you, because he'd likely stop here for some smithy work. Are you saying you saw him?"

"Him or his twin brother," the blacksmith answered. "He stopped here just like you did, to ask about trails. I'm right sure it's the fellow you're after, because I didn't like the way he talked nor acted. It wasn't that he had the look of a brand-buster or an outlaw, but I seen right away that the horse he was on and his led horse both looked like he'd been chousing 'em pretty hard."

"And you'd be a man who could tell that for sure," Longarm stated. "But just so I don't make a mistake about him being the one I'm after, maybe you'd best tell me a little bit more about him."

"Big fellow he was, and real short-spoken," the smith said. "And he had a scar or tattoo mark of some kind on one hand. Closest way I can tell you what it was like, I'd say it might've been a J."

"If it curved like a J and you didn't get but a quick look at it, you might've taken it to be a fishhook?"

"I'd say you could call it that," the blacksmith answered. "But you'd likely have to look at it twice to be sure which it was, and even then it'd be a toss-up."

"Well, you've just said what I was hoping you would," Longarm told the blacksmith. "On account of it fits the man I'm after right down to a T. Now I got another question to ask you. Did this fellow have much of anything to say to you? I mean about where he'd been or who he was or where he might be heading?"

"He didn't say anything about who he was or where he come from. All he asked me was a few questions about the easiest and shortest way from here to Medford. If I was a betting man, I'd lay ten to one that's where he was heading. On the other hand . . ." The blacksmith paused. "Stolen gold, you say?"

"Two sacks of stolen gold."

The blacksmith nodded. "In that case it wouldn't be Medford."

"Why not?" Longarm asked.

"First off, if it's got something to do with gold, it ain't Medford he'd be after. He'd want to turn off to Jacksonville, which is about four or five miles away from Medford. That's where the gold smelter is."

"How big of a place is this Jacksonville?" Longarm asked.

"Last time I visited down thataway it sure wasn't big as it used to be. About all that's left there is the big smelter and the Beekman Bank."

"You talk like you're pretty well acquainted with that part of the country," Longarm said.

"Sure I am. It's because I started working in Jacksonville when I was about knee high to a duck. The first job I ever worked at was water boy in the gold smelter there. Watching the smelter-hands work gold is what got me into blacksmithing."

"Then you'd be sure the smelter's still there?" Longarm frowned. "I don't know much about the country thereabouts."

Scratching his chin, the blacksmith replied, "Well, the the last time I visited down thataway was about a month or so ago, and the smelter and the Beekman Bank was still doing business. Why, both of 'em has been there longer'n most folks recall. I guess there's bigger smelters down the coast in California, in the Gold Rush country, but the one I'm talking about is a pretty good-sized one."

"Well, what's the best road to take that'll get me to Jacksonville?"

"Well, there ain't all that many roads hereabouts to bother you. If you come right down to it, there's not any real roads, but there's a pretty good bunch of trails that runs all crisscross to the main trail. If I was in your shoes, I'd just keep pushing on a mite south of west."

"You figure I might make it before dark?" Longarm asked.

"It's not much of a chance, but there's not any law that says you can't try. I haven't been over that trail for a month or more, but little creeks is all you'll have to ford, and there's a place or two along the way where you can rent a bed for the night."

"That sounds right good, and I thank you for all your help," Longarm said. "Now if I want to make any time in what's left of daylight, I better be leaving. The clouds are piling up, and I'd bet there's rain ahead."

"There almost always is," the smith said. "Except for the last two days, it's been coming down pretty good. But if you watch your p's and q's you can cross all the little creeks you'll run into, even if they do look mean."

Longarm glanced at the saloon as he left the smithy. He considered the idea of dropping in for a drink, but shook his head and went to his horse. Mounting, he reined away from the little settlement and started for the trail. Following the sketchy directions he'd been given, when he came to the first fork in the trail he reined to the one branching off to the southwest and settled down for the long ride that stretched ahead of him.

● ● ●

The glistening haze of raindrops had stopped falling shortly before sunset, and Longarm scanned the trail ahead. He made no effort to toe his horse into a faster gait, knowing that his mount was as tired as he was himself. He'd already discovered that footing on the rain-drenched trail was treacherous. There had been several times during his long ride when Longarm had been forced to dismount and wade almost boot-top deep in order to lead his balking horse across one of the huge puddles that blocked the trail.

Once again, the horse balked as it encountered a puddle the size of a small lake covering the trail. Longarm drummed his heels on its flanks and slapped its rump, trying to force it to cross the roiled swirling pool. The animal remained stubbornly motionless at the water's edge, its only move the tossing of its head. Voice commands had no effect on the stubborn animal, nor did rump-slaps and heel-bumps.

"Old son," Longarm muttered to himself, "this damnfool critter ain't about to go no further unless you drag him, and it ain't going to be no easier to back him up than it'd be to push ahead. Looks like the only way to get him across this puddle is to lead him."

Longarm managed to take off his boots while still on his horse's back. He tied the boots to the front saddlestrings, then levered out of the saddle, standing with one foot in a stirrup. When he lowered his free foot into the puddle, the ice-cold water filled the leg of his jeans and chilled him thoroughly.

Once he felt bottom with the foot he'd advanced, he brought down his other leg. The chill of the water surrounded it, and now both his legs felt the same icy shock. Longarm stretched to reach the reins of his horse, caught them in a firm grip, and started leading the animal across the miniature lake. Knowing that his feet would quickly

103

become numb, he moved as quickly as possible across the rock-studded bottom.

Longarm quickly grew accustomed to the cold swirling water. He was able to reach the opposite side of the puddle without getting more than a few icy splashes on his face when the horse resisted being led.

Mounted again, he made good time along the rain-drenched trail for perhaps a half mile before encountering another water-crossing. Aware that no two crossings would be the same, Longarm reined in to study the surface of the water beyond the point where it flowed across the road. He did not like what he saw in the moonlight. Not only was this crossing wider than the previous one, it had a flowing current that created large patches of white foaming bubbles.

"Now, this damn place looks like it's apt to be a mite more trouble than that last one," Longarm muttered as he took out a fresh cheroot and lighted it. "But if it ain't got too deep of a drop in the bottom, you can get across it. Then maybe the rest of the way'll be easier on you and the horse both."

After he'd looked around in the moonlight for several moments, Longarm decided that he would find no easy course. He tugged at the halter strap to bring the horse closer to him and started picking his way forward. Now he moved only one short careful step at a time, pausing at the end of each advance to tighten his grip on the reins to urge the animal toward the opposite bank.

Picking his way blindly, guided only by feeling the bottom with his already numbed feet, Longarm began to lead the horse through the expanse of moonlit water that stretched ahead. When he reached the center of the huge puddle Longarm felt the current of the big pool's feeder stream pushing against his legs. The surface ripples were only inches below his crotch now, and once or twice his bare feet almost slipped from a boulder on which he was trying to plant them.

Soon he passed the center of the rippling surface. Taking a firmer grip on the stirrup strap, he advanced his foot carefully. He moved it in an arc from side to side and stretched to the utmost as he sought another solid surface that would support him while making his next step.

At last Longarm was sure he'd found the rock for which he'd been searching. The side of his bare foot had scraped against the rock only lightly as he moved his foot slowly over it. He found that it had a flatter, rougher surface than the others he'd touched in his underwater probing. Then, when he put his full weight on the rock, he realized belatedly that with his sense of feeling numbed by the icy water he'd chosen a teeter-totter stone that reacted to his weight like a rocking chair.

As the stone shifted back and forth, the icy water engulfed Longarm's legs to mid-thigh. All that he could do was keep his precarious balance and cling to the reins as he teetered and tottered and tugged as gently as possible on the reins while hoping the animal would obey the light pulls he was giving them. After what seemed a very long time the horse responded. It stepped slowly up to Longarm, and stood quietly while Longarm scrabbled from the rock into the saddle.

"You done just fine that time," Longarm said aloud as he toed the horse ahead. "Now maybe we can get the rest of the way without having to freeze our butts off again."

Soon he reached the other side of the water. Although the cool air rippled up inside the cloth of his wet cold jeans and crept up the insides of their legs, Longarm did not stop to put on his boots. He tried to forget the chill of his water-soaked trousers as they brushed his legs, but when he reached the next stretch of down-slope he could see nothing at its bottom but the occasional glints of moonlight reflected from the tumbling surface of rushing water.

"Somebody oughta have sense enough to build a bridge or two along this trail," he muttered. "A man that's in a hurry loses a lot of time when he's got to do some wading and lead a horse across these damn little river-shoots."

Longarm began studying the stream's roiling surface as the horse descended the gentle slope. As he drew closer to its edge he breathed a sigh of relief and reined to a halt. The crossing he'd reached this time was not a pool, but a broad expanse of shallow tumbling currents, the water splitting into blobbed white shoots where its flow was parted by protruding rocks.

Then as Longarm watched the stream more carefully, shifting his gaze from point to point, he began to make out a pattern of wide stretches where gentle currents flowed. Nodding with satisfaction, he toed the horse ahead. Glancing down after it had moved forward a short distance, he could see the animal's knees above the shining surface of the water. Taking advantage of his discovery, he divided his attention between the distant dark line of the horizon and the water's edge ahead.

"You're lucky there ain't no wind blowing right now, old son," Longarm muttered to himself. "Because just as sure as God made little green apples you'd be frozen by now. But you'd best be a mite more careful, because this ain't the time or the place for you to take a bath."

At last his zigzag passage brought him to the opposite side of the stretch of white-streaked dancing water. The horse plodded up the long slant away from the stream, its hooves grating on earth. Even in the moonlight Longarm could see stretches of the trail between thin stands of timber.

Before he'd covered a great deal of ground the character of the trail changed; it became a hard-beaten graveled path, much wider than before. A few wagon-ruts appeared now, old marks of journeys long past faintly visible in the moonlight.

"Looks like you're about to get where you're heading, old son," Longarm told himself, speaking aloud. "And it ain't a bit too soon, because you're a lot hungrier than you are sleepy. Was a horse to stray across the road right now, you'd be hard put not to try and make a sandwich outa it."

Chapter 10

Longarm reined in to rest his horse when he reached the end of the high stands of thick brush and tall trees that had lined both sides of the trail. So far the only signs of human habitation had been the widely scattered wrecked ruins of a few small cabins. While he was taking out a cigar and lighting it, Longarm studied the more open country that stretched ahead in the moonlight. There was less timbered land on both sides of the trail, and the narrow beaten path ran straighter now than it had only a short time earlier.

"Now, that sure don't look like the country you been riding through, old son," he said aloud as he exhaled a small burst of smoke. "But it's the only trail there is, and there's got to be someplace up ahead where there's people a man can talk to and get straightened around on how to get to the place you're headed for."

Touching the horse's flank with the toe of his boot to speed up its lagging progress, Longarm kept his eyes on the trail ahead, an easy enough chore in the moonlight. He rounded a long sweeping curve, and on a straight stretch of road ahead saw a welcome brightness of yellow that glittered through the sparse roadside growth. As he drew closer he could see the black bulk of a building ahead behind the brightness, and a few moments later saw a dimmer glow that came from a shaded window near the back of the building.

Though it seemed to him that he'd never reach the promising light, at last he came abreast of a small open area where he pulled reins to bring his horse to a halt in front of bulking outlines of a two-story building and some outbuildings at the back of the open space. Above the wide front door there was a weather-beaten sign illuminated by the lantern which had been his beacon. "Travelers' Rest," it read. "Rooms and Meals."

"You can use a lot of all three of them things," Longarm said into the quiet air. "And it don't look like you'll have to rouse anybody up. Folks that's asleep have already put out their lights, and it ain't likely that whoever's inside there'd leave 'em burning after they've gone off to bed."

Swinging out of his saddle, Longarm stepped to the door of the inn and tried the knob. It did not turn, and he rapped on the door with his knuckles. Several minutes passed, and Longarm was getting a bit restive in the cool night breeze that crept through his still-moist clothing when he heard footsteps approaching the door. It opened to reveal a wizened, stoop-shouldered man, who stepped out to stand in the rectangle of light streaming from inside. He was wearing bib overalls over a suit of red-flannel underwear.

For a moment he stood without speaking, looking at Longarm's wet and bedraggled clothing. Then he bobbed his head and said, "Evening, friend. I'll tell you right off that you got here just at the right time. I was getting ready to close up."

"I'd have liked it better myself if I'd got here sooner,"

Longarm replied. "That trail's meaner'n a raw bronco getting rode for the first time."

"It looks to me like you got caught in the rain back along the trail and didn't have time to find cover. Why don't you come inside where you can be comfortable?"

"Now, I'm going to take your invite and come inside soon as I can," he told the man. "Because this is the first place I've come to where it looks like a traveler can find a bed for the night."

"I take it you're figuring on stopping here then?"

"I sure am," Longarm replied.

"Well, you're more'n welcome, stranger. We got plenty of rooms and all of 'em are vacant."

"I'd imagine you got a barn where there'll be a stall for my horse?"

"Of course I do," the man replied. "But before you start settling in, I reckon I'd better tell you that a room's going to cost you a half-dollar a night, and it'll be a dime extra for the horse and his feed."

"That sounds fair enough," Longarm said. "And I could use a bite to eat myself. All I've had to chew on are saddle rations. These past few miles my belly's been telling me it thinks my throat's been cut."

"If you don't mind taking potluck, I can manage a meal for you. That is, if you ain't too picky. Meals cost two bits."

"Fair enough," Longarm said. "Now, my name's Long, Custis Long. I'm a deputy U.S. marshal out this way on a case, so you don't have to worry about getting paid however much I'd owe you. If you'd like to see my badge—"

"You wouldn't tell me who you are unless it was true," the man broke in. "Or offer to show me your badge. My name's Edmonds, Mart Edmonds, and I welcome you to Travelers' Rest."

"Well, then," Longarm went on, "if you'll just head me out to where your barn is, I'll lead my horse to it and get his saddle off. If you got some empty burlap sacks, like in most barns, I'll borrow one with your permission so I can rub him down a mite before I come inside to settle for the night."

"You'll find the stable right around back," the innkeeper said. "But leading your horse to it's a job I'll be glad to take care of for you, along with tossing some hay for him into the feed trough. The way you look now, you need to rest a lot worse than your horse does."

"I take your offer right kindly," Longarm replied. "But there ain't much use in you having to pull on boots and traipse outside for a little chore like that."

"It don't bother me a bit," the man said.

Longarm raised his hand. "I ain't just being polite. The sooner you start fixing my grub, the quicker I'll be eating it. Let's settle for me tending to the horse and you lending me a lantern, in case you got one handy."

"If that's the way you want it to be," Edmonds said. "There's a lantern on the back stoop, and I'd imagine you've got a match. While you're looking after your horse, I'll go open the back door so you can come in by it. You look like you could use a good hot cup of coffee while I get your supper ready, and there's a pot just fresh on the kitchen stove."

"Now, that's an offer I was hoping you'd make," Longarm told him. "And after I get my horse unsaddled and set with some hay, I'll be joining up with you quicker'n you can say Jack Robinson."

Longarm made a quick job of unsaddling and giving his bedraggled mount a good rubdown. Tossing his saddlebags over his shoulder, he made his way to the back door. As the innkeeper had promised, the door stood slightly ajar, and

Longarm stepped through it into a wave of warm air coming from the big cookstove near the doorway. Longarm wasted no time in stepping close to the stove. He was rubbing his hands above it, feeling their sensitivity return, when Edmonds came in.

"I thought I'd find you back here getting warm," he said. "Oregon's fine country, Marshal Long, but here in the Klamath country it does get raw and cold when the wind's from the north or west, specially when it brings a big rain with it. The weather's been pretty bad for several days now, but you'd know that better than me, traveling here in it."

"I'll double that in spades," Longarm agreed. "I've been out in it long enough. But a man in my job's got to do what he's paid for, whether it's rain or shine."

"I can understand that," Edmonds said. "But if you're not too tired to sit down for a while in an easy chair in front of a fireplace, I'll just show you into the parlor room where you can get your feet warm and dry off a bit. I've already put some victuals on the stove to warm up for you. You can eat in the room I'll be taking you to. Just come along with me."

"Now, that's an invite I can't turn down," Longarm told the innkeeper. "You lead the way and I won't be far behind you."

Longarm followed the innkeeper into a large room that despite its obvious years of hard use retained an air of gracefulness. A large Oriental rug, threads protruding from it in several places, covered most of the floor.

It was furnished with a mixture of leather-upholstered lounge chairs, straight-backed kitchen chairs, and a few cushion-seat rocking chairs. A large table stood in its center, the top scored with scratches and dents. A fireplace holding a dying bed of coals occupied most of the outer wall, with two easy chairs on either side of it.

Edmonds gestured toward the fireplace as he said, "Take your choice, Marshal Long. A chair by the fire's fine, but your victuals ought to be warmed up by now, and I'd imagine you'll want to eat at the table."

"It don't make no never-mind to me," Longarm said. "But I'm hungrier than I am cold, so I'll sit at the table to eat and then move up by the fire, if it's all the same to you."

"Whatever you say," Edmonds answered. He was disappearing through the door as he spoke. "It won't take me but a minute to serve up. I know how hungry a man can get when he's been out in Oregon weather on a cold night."

Longarm had just gotten comfortably seated in one of the straight-back chairs beside the table when the innkeeper returned carrying a tray. He placed it in front of Longarm and said, "It's a long ways from being a feast, but it'll fill your belly and warm you up, so just dig in. I'll tend the fire while you're eating, and go back after the coffeepot as soon as it hottens up."

Longarm nodded his thanks as he began to cut into bite-sized pieces the thick slab of roast beef that was on the plate, together with a mound of mashed potatoes and a scant helping of beans. The innkeeper watched him for a moment before leaving again. Longarm ate hungrily, and had almost cleaned his plate when Edmonds returned, carrying a steaming coffeepot and cups.

"If I don't tell you now I might forget later," he said. "It looks like you're the only one who'll be stopping here tonight, so I've put a candle for you on the little stand by the stairway. When you're ready for bed, just go up the stairs and pick out any room that looks good to you."

"Well, I need to get all my travel-kinks worked out before I turn in," Longarm replied. "So I aim to set a while, till after I've finished my coffee and smoked down my cigar."

"Then if you don't mind, I'll just drink a cup of coffee with you," Edmonds told Longarm. "A man oughtn't go to bed too soon after he's had a meal, so that'll be a good way to pass a bit of time." He hesitated for a moment. "If that's all right with you, Marshal Long. I ought't've asked you first."

"Why, I don't go much on hemming and hawing myself," Longarm replied after he'd swallowed the bite of roast beef he'd been chewing. "And I was aiming to ask you if you'd mind setting here with me a little while. It's been a long spell since I had a case bring me to these parts, and then I was mostly just traveling through. There's a few questions I'd sure like to ask you, if you don't mind."

"Why, I'll be glad to. I'll tend the fire, put on a fresh log, and when you've finished eating we'll visit."

While the innkeeper was adding a fresh log to the fire Longarm finished his meal. He pushed the plate back and stood up. Edmonds gestured toward an easy chair at one side of the hearth, and settled down in its mate on the opposite side. Longarm dropped into the chair the innkeeper had indicated, and after he'd stretched out his legs he lighted a cigar.

"I got to admit that it's a lot better sitting here than forking a horse out in that cold wind I been riding in," he said. "But I'm after a real bad outlaw and lallygagging ain't something I can afford to do."

"I hope you're catching up with him," Edmonds said.

"Oh, I'll run him down. Come to think of it, it just might be he stopped off here. You recall a big fellow, mean-looking, heading west? He was probably riding a roan, and leading a dun that was toting a real heavy load."

For a moment the innkeeper was silent. Then he said, "I

wouldn't want to steer you wrong, Marshal Long. But let's see, it was three days ago that a big heavyset man with a led horse stopped here for the night. The led horse was close to being foundered, it didn't have much go left in it. Seems to me the led horse was a dun, and the fellow was riding a roan."

"Which way was he heading?"

"Toward Jacksonville, he said. He asked a few questions."

"Questions like what?" Longarm asked.

"About the road that'd get him to Jacksonville the quickest. And about the smelter and the Beekman Bank there."

"Did you tell him what he wanted to know?"

"Sure did. It just happens that I grew up in Jacksonville. It's not a long ways from here, just a few hours' ride. The gold deposits are just about played out by now, but the smelter's still going pretty fair."

"How does it manage to keep going if there's not all that much gold being dug?"

"I'd imagine it's on account of there's not all that many smelters north of the big California gold fields, but there's still a lot of prospectors poking around up to the north and east."

"Prospectors are still bringing ore to it?"

"Oh, sure. It's a lot closer than the ones they'd have to go to in California."

"I can see that," Longarm said.

"And the Beekman Bank is still open," Edmonds went on. "Being as it was the first big one anyplace close, the Beekman brothers got enough of a start to hold out pretty good."

"And their bank's still doing business, like the smelter?"

"It's still in business, but they started a branch in Medford

116

when things got to tapering off in Jacksonville. Both of the Beekman boys are dead now, but their hired men are still running the banks."

"From what you've said, Jacksonville's not such a much of a place now," Longarm said.

"Well, it's not what it used to be, and that's for sure. Why, when it was booming there was houses all over and several hotels. But all the hotels are mostly gone now or run down. When you come right down to it, my place is about the only decent one between Medford and Klamath Falls where travelers to the east and west both can get a bed for the night and a meal."

"And you've been here quite a spell?"

"Well, the place has, but I haven't. I guess you'd have to call me a Johnny-come-lately in this kind of work. But I been in this part of the country most of my life." Edmonds smiled. "I remember when the first gold strike was made on what they call Gold Hill now; that happened when I was a boy. But I was old enough to watch the bricklayers putting up the first smelter after word got around about that gold strike. And when I was just a youngster the Beekman brothers started their bank, a big brick building, the biggest building except the smelter anybody in those parts had ever seen."

Longarm held up a hand to stop Edmonds. "It ain't that I don't want to hear your story, but what I need to know right now is if you're acquainted with whoever's in charge of that smelter."

"You'd be meaning Clem Simpson. Sure, I've known him a long time. I go in and swap lies a while with him when I get into town. Clem generally ain't all that busy any longer. In the old days the smelter had nigh onto sixty or seventy men working it. Now there's only fifteen, sometimes twenty."

117

"I'd take it that you know most of 'em?"

"Oh, sure. They're all good men, old-timers. They're about all the folks I know in Jacksonville now."

"Well, I got to say that what-all you've told me gives me a lot of ideas," Longarm went on. "But now that I've got warmed up, right this minute I'm beginning to get more'n a mite sleepy. If you don't mind waiting till after breakfast in the morning to go on with what we just been talking about, I'd sure feel a lot more like listening."

"Why, of course you're tired," Edmonds said. "But you know how us old codgers are. Once we get started on talking about old times, we just sort of ramble on."

"I wouldn't say you've done much rambling." Longarm smiled. "And I got to tell you, what you said has helped me a lot."

"That makes me feel some better, but now I'll just say good night, Marshal. You're welcome to sit here and enjoy the fire as long as you feel like it, but if I was you, I'd go to bed and get that sleep you're needing."

"And that's what I aim to do soon as I smoke down my cigar," Longarm said.

"I've put a candlestick on the desk outside, it'll get you up to your room," Edmonds told him. "I imagine you'll be heading out early tomorrow."

"Maybe not," said Longarm. "I want to talk more about Jacksonville. And my horse could use the extra rest. We'll see in the morning."

After the innkeeper had left, Longarm sat by the fire for a short while, until his cheroot had burned down to a stub. He tossed it onto the dying coals in the fireplace and stepped out of the room. His saddlebags and rifle rested at the foot of the stairs, and on a small table nearby was the candle the innkeeper had mentioned.

Picking up his gear in one hand, Longarm took the

candlestick in the other and mounted the stairway. A narrow corridor lined with open doorways stretched in front of him. He turned into the nearest, dropped his gear just inside the door, and put the candlestick on a small table that stood against the wall near the bed.

Levering out of his boots, Longarm stripped quickly and placed his Colt on the table beside the bed. Then he stretched out and wriggled around to find the areas which had the smallest lumps, but before he'd finished seeking the softest spots he'd fallen asleep.

Chapter 11

Quite unexpectedly Longarm reached a fork in the trail and reined his horse in. Settling back in his saddle, he lighted a cheroot and studied his surroundings. He'd left the Travelers' Rest around noon, hoping that by late afternoon he'd reach Jacksonville. Rested by the stop at the inn beside the trail, Longarm had started out that day with a new vigor. His horse had shown by its friskiness during the ride that its own rest had restored the animal's resilience, just as it had his own.

Longarm had not pushed his horse on the stretch of ground he'd covered since leaving the Travelers' Rest. He'd been satisfied to let the animal set its own gait, but had kept it moving steadily. After his talk with Mart Edmonds he'd been more certain than ever that the obvious destination for the fleeing Wilson and the packhorse he was leading was the smelter at Jacksonville. Now he stared at the trail-fork.

Accustomed to using sky-signs as both timekeeper and guide, Longarm glanced up at the cloudless blue sky. When he saw that the blazing sun was more than halfway toward the horizon, he smiled and said into the quiet air, "Old son, Lady Luck was sure sitting on your shoulder when you stopped at that old fellow's place last night. There ain't nothing that'll help a man to think right like sleeping all night in a real bed and setting down to a hot breakfast and lunch before you hit the trail again."

Longarm's musings had not distracted his attention from the trail; he'd been studying its hoof-pocked surface since reining in, scanning the ground where the trail branched. Even without dismounting he could see that its right-hand fork bore more signs of recent use than did the one on the left. Settling back, Longarm studied the up-slope ahead of him.

"Now, that's a real funny thing," he muttered. "That Edmonds fellow didn't say a word about this trail splitting. But it's real easy to see that the left-hand fork ain't such a much, it ain't been used like the other one. Now, that can't mean but one thing. The right-handed branch has got to go to Medford. What you just better do, old son, is go up along the left-handed one and see if it don't get you to Jacksonville and that smelter."

There was little space atop the crest of the long rise, and its limited surface was quite literally covered with a maze of hoofprints. Many of the prints had been eroded by time and the assaults of Oregon's frequent rains. Longarm sat in the saddle for a moment while he scanned the small flattened area, looking for the tracks left by Wilson's heavily laden packhorse. These more deeply incised prints had been the chief guide he'd followed since taking up his chase after the gold thief.

Longarm soon found the tracks he was seeking. Even among the confusion of prints in the soft yielding soil, dozens of sets of old and half-obliterated hoofprints at the trail-fork, the deeply set tracks left by the led horse loaded with stolen gold were unmistakable.

He had no trouble in identifying the clear crescent-shaped depressions of the hooves of the horse carrying the sacks of double eagles; they could not be mistaken for those of a horse burdened with only a rider. Longarm followed the prints quite easily as he descended, and kept them in sight at the bottom of the rise.

"Well, thanks to that nice old gent that runs the place you spent the night at, you don't need to fret any longer, old son," Longarm told himself. "Now, you can be certain-sure about which way to head and catch up with that gold thief. The big question is, are you going to get to that smelter at Jacksonville before those bags of double eagles get dumped into the melting-furnace?" Nodding with satisfaction, Longarm urged his mount to a faster pace.

After a while he breathed a sigh of relief when one of his intermittent glances at the distant horizon-line showed that it was no longer level. In the distance and to the south and west of the trail the rounded bulge of a huge low hill was beginning to take recognizable shape. Longarm reined in and studied the changed horizon for a moment before smiling.

"Old son, you must've been listening better'n you figured you was when that Mart Edmonds fellow was talking, because the hump up ahead there has got to be the one he told you about, Timber Mountain. And if Edmonds was right, Jacksonville can't be much more'n two or three miles ahead, cuddled down on a level stretch right in front of it."

Feeling encouraged because the end of his long chase was now in sight, Longarm poked his horse's flank with a boot toe. The horse moved ahead once more, and Longarm settled back into a more comfortable position in his saddle, watching the changing horizon-line. The trail circled now in a much more pronounced curve; then, after another mile or two, its slope suddenly became string-straight for a short distance up the slanting side of a high bluff.

Longarm reached the crest of the rise and found himself looking down on a half mile of trail that disappeared in a clutter of small houses. Beyond them, in the distance, were the high brick walls of a circular building. Longarm was certain that the building was the smelter, though no smoke trails rose from its array of chimneys.

Immediately below him the zigzag trail cut its way down a steep slope, onto the narrow expanse of level ground below, where the trail stretched string-straight again before ending at the settlement.

"You know, old son, if this was a poker game you'd say it was getting real close to calling time," Longarm said, his voice breaking the total silence of the clear air. "And you still don't know what kinda hand you drew, so you better not waste too much time before taking a look at your cards."

Reining his mount into motion, Longarm let it pick its own way down the sharp bends in the trail. The horse balked only a time or two when it was faced with a short steep stretch where it had to slide a few paces with stiffened forelegs, but sooner than Longarm had anticipated, the animal came to a halt at the base of the slope. It stood quietly for a few moments; then Longarm dug a boot toe into its flank and nudged it ahead.

When Longarm had first seen the town laid out below him like a map, it had been obvious to him that there was only one place where he should go before heading for the smelter. He picked his way through the narrow streets of the little town to the building that dominated the main street.

Long before he reached the imposing structure Longarm could read the gilt-lettered words "Beekman Bank" on the building's facade. Looping the reins of his horse over the hitch rail in front of it, Longarm went inside.

At his first glimpse of the building's interior Longarm got the impression that it housed a shrine rather than a bank. Its floor was made from marble slabs, and the same material had been used for the chest-high counters, which were broken by gilt columns to divide them into tellers' windows.

A few faint voices rose from the windows, which were the main feature of the building's interior, along with a large section just past the entrance where polished oak and mahogany desks stood spaced widely apart. There were small gaggles of men in front of most of the tellers' windows, but the black-garbed men stationed at the neat rows of desks worked individually and in silence.

Longarm had stopped a step or two inside the door, and when a man at one of the closer desks looked up and saw him, the man rose and came to the door. Stopping in front of Longarm he said, "I don't recall having seen you here in the bank before, sir. Can I be of assistance?"

"I guess I didn't figure this place to be big as it is," Longarm replied.

As he spoke, Longarm was taking out the wallet which contained his badge. He flipped it open and showed the badge to the man in front of him.

Before the banker could say anything more, Longarm went on. "Now, maybe you can tell me who I'd need to talk to. My name's Long, Custis Long. Like it says on my badge, I'm a deputy United States marshal outa the Denver office, and the case I'm working on is why I'm here."

"I'll be very happy to do anything I can to help you, Marshal Long," the banker said. "My name is Forbes, James Forbes. I think I can answer any questions you might care to ask."

"Glad to make your acquaintance," Longarm said. "Now, maybe you've heard about the fellow that owned a bank up in Grant's Pass getting killed? His name was Shaw."

"Yes, of course," Forbes replied. "I'd never met him myself, but I'm familiar with the names of most of the bankers here in Oregon. Mr. Shaw was shot, or so I've heard. I'm not familiar with all the details of his death."

"Well, you heard right about him being shot," Longarm said. "But before we go on palavering right out here where anybody might catch some of what I need to talk to you about, I think we better find a place where we can talk in private."

"Suppose we step into one of our client consultation rooms," the banker suggested, gesturing toward a small enclosed cubicle by one of the walls. "What you have to tell me won't be overheard by anyone."

Without waiting for Longarm to reply, Forbes started moving toward the little enclosure. Longarm hurried after him, and stepped into the cubicle as the banker opened its door. Glass panels in three sides and the roof of the small enclosure made it as well-lighted as the rest of the building's interior. The cubbyhole contained a pair of chairs with a wide shelf between them. Longarm settled down into the chair the banker indicated, and waited until the bank official sat down across from him.

"I must admit that I'm quite interested in anything you might have to tell me about Mr. Shaw's death," Forbes said. "I suppose he was killed during a bank holdup?"

"It wasn't anything like that," Longarm replied. "But going by what you just asked me, I don't imagine you've heard that it was one of Shaw's own men that shot him?"

Forbes's jaw dropped and his eyes opened wide as he stared across the shelf at Longarm. Then he asked, "Was the man who killed him insane? Or had he been caught embezzling from Mr. Shaw's bank?"

"Neither one," Longarm replied. "Shaw and the fellow that killed him—his name's Wilson, as near as I've been able to find out—were in cahoots. Both of 'em were crooks, and I don't have any idea right yet how much stealing they were doing. What's brought me here on Wilson's trail is that he's stolen two big sacks of double eagles from the U.S. Government. My job's to catch up with him and get that loot back."

Forbes had recovered his poised air by the time Longarm completed his explanation. Now he said, "I think I see the picture clearly, Marshal Long. Isn't it your belief that the miscreant you're after has come here because of the smelter?"

"That's exactly what I got in mind," Longarm told him. "Gold bars are worth just about the same as gold that's been through the U.S. Mint, and sure as God made little green apples, once those double eagles are melted into bars, there ain't no way in the world for anybody to prove they used to be Uncle Sam's double eagles."

"Yes, that's the same thought that occurred to me," Forbes said. He sat for a moment in silent thought. "But if this thief you're after is counting on having his loot melted down here in Jacksonville, he's going to be a very disappointed man. The smelter's been closed down for a week now, and still is closed."

"I hope you ain't saying it's shut down for good!" Longarm exclaimed.

"Oh, no. Nothing like that. It's needed some repair work for quite a while. As soon as everything's been fixed it'll open again."

"Now, that's about the best news you could give me," Longarm said. "But how much longer's it going to be till it's back in business?"

"Another week, perhaps a bit longer," Forbes replied. "I'd say that if you do some looking around right here in town you've got a pretty good chance of running your man to earth."

"Oh, that idea's occurred to me," Longarm said. "I don't reckon there's any more smelters close by where he'd be able to take that gold he stole?"

"He'd have to make a very long trip," Forbes said. "During the gold rush in these parts—which I'm sure you know didn't last very long—there were three smelters close by, including the one here. But now there's not another gold smelter left in business between here and San Francisco."

"And there ain't none back to the north, that much I know," Longarm said thoughtfully.

"You're right, of course," Forbes said.

Longarm shook his head. "You know, I just don't see this fellow I'm after doing all that much traveling. He's been on the trail as long as I have, and my guess is he'll settle down here and wait for the smelter to start up again. And that's going to give me a chance to run him down."

"If there's any way that we at the Beekman Bank can help you . . ." Forbes began. He fell silent when Longarm shook his head and stood up.

Longarm said, "This thief I'm after just might come in here, so I better tell you what he looks like. He's a big man, dark-haired, and if you look close at his right hand you'll see a sorta old scarred tattoo mark, looks something like a fishhook."

"I'll caution our people, tell them to be on the lookout too," Forbes promised. "And as I was about to say, if we here at the bank can help you—"

Longarm broke in. "Outside of telling me which'd be the best hotel or boardinghouse where I can put up, and letting me know if you hear anything about that Wilson fellow, there ain't much of anything anybody can do."

Forbes paused. "The hotels here—well, I'd hesitate to recommend any of them. I've heard that Mrs. Morton's boardinghouse over on Elm Street is about the best in town, if she's got a room to rent right now. Her place is just down the street a little way, you can't miss it."

"Well, I do thank you for your help," Longarm said. "And it might be I'll need to ask you another question or two, if I come across something that puzzles me. But right now, I'm aiming to mosey around a bit before I decide on a place to settle into while I'm here, maybe go out to the smelter first and see when they plan to open it up again."

"Well, Marshal Long, if anyone we don't know comes into the bank to make a big deposit of gold coins, I'm sure we can manage to get word to you. And if you should need any help in finding your way around, or for anything else, please feel free to call on us."

"Now, that's a mighty nice offer, but I hope I don't have to bother you any more. I'll just find a place to stay, and then I'll let you know where it is, so if you do have somebody come in like you said, you'll know where to find me. But first I'll just mosey on out to the smelter."

"Ask for Clem Simpson, he's the smelter's boss-man," Forbes suggested. "And if you mention that you stopped to talk with us here at the bank, it might not do any harm."

"Well, I'll sure keep that in mind," Longarm promised. "Now, I know you got work to do, so I'll just mosey along and see what else I can find out."

Outside again in the sparkling clear air, Longarm mounted and reined his horse ahead. He followed a zigzag course through the town, locating Jacksonville's saloon row and riding the length of its small business district before reining his horse toward the idled smelter.

Chapter 12

Longarm rode toward the smelter. Now, with the sun beginning to drop toward the horizon, the building he was approaching looked like nothing so much as a huge dark round brick blob. It lacked corners of any kind, and as he drew still closer Longarm realized that the strange structure was much larger than it had seemed to be when he'd first sighted it.

A number of short smokestacks rose from the building's domed roof; Longarm counted eight of them. Soon he could also see that while the building's walls had been built of oversized bricks, its high blank yellowish-brown surface was broken at intervals by silvery strips that rose from the ground to the structure's roof. As he progressed still further, he realized that the silvery strips must be glass windows. He could not see any sign of a door.

Longarm took a cigar from his vest pocket, lighted it, and exhaled a puff or two of smoke as he continued to study the flat terrain as well as the building ahead. The path his horse was following did not run straight now. It was a strip of raw grassless soil winding sinuously between the surface of cracked dried-up mud puddles that as nearly as he could tell encircled the building.

Longarm spoke aloud. "That damnfool place looks a lot more like a fort or maybe a jail than it does a smelter."

Toeing his horse ahead, Longarm now advanced to within a half-dozen yards of the strange-looking building. He reined in and sat for a moment leaning back in his saddle, scanning the blank featureless curving wall of the big squat structure, trying to find something that looked like a door. Even at the point where the little path ended at the smelter's wall, there was no sign of a door.

"Looks like here's where the path stops, old son," he said aloud. "And that's bound to mean that somewhere close around here there's a way for a man to get inside of that funny-looking place, even if it don't seem like there is. The only thing you got to do now is find it."

Twitching the reins of his horse to start it moving again, Longarm was lifting the leathers to swing his horse around and ride along the perimeter of the building when a grating noise sounded from inside it. In a moment the shining opaque panel in front of him began sliding slowly to one side. Tightening his reins quickly to stop the horse, Longarm cocked his head, trying to look into the building. Before he could really see anything of its interior, the panel stopped sliding and a tall husky man stepped through the opening. He was holding a rifle in the crook of his arm.

"Smelter's still closed," he said. "So if you've got a refining job for us, you'll just have to wait until we're ready to stoke up again."

"Oh, I ain't bringing no ore for you to melt down," Longarm assured him. "But there's some business I need to talk about with your boss."

"Start talking then," the man said. "I'm the boss."

"You're Clem Simpson, I guess?" Longarm asked. Before

the man in the opening had a chance to reply he went on. "My name's Long, Custis Long. I'm a deputy U.S. marshal outa the Denver office. If you want me to show you my badge, I'll be glad to, but I'd like to be sure you won't figure I'm reaching to draw a gun on you before I move."

"My name's Clem Simpson," the man replied. He made no move to raise the rifle's muzzle. "And you're right about me wanting to get a look at your badge."

"I figured you would," Longarm said. "Now, I got to reach into my pocket to get my wallet. I'll take it real kindly if you'll just keep that Winchester's muzzle still when I start to pull it out."

Simpson dropped the rifle's muzzle until it was pointing to the ground and cocked his head as an invitation for Longarm to move. Sliding his wallet from his pocket, Longarm spread it open and held it down for the smelter's boss to look at the badge pinned to its inside fold. After he'd inspected the badge, Simpson nodded and stepped aside from the opening in the building's wall.

"I'm sorry I felt like I had to come out carrying my rifle," Simpson said. "But there's always a chance that some outlaw bunch is waiting to rob this place. It's happened a time or two, but the outlaws have left us alone since we put up this building that looks like it doesn't have any doors."

"Well, sir, it sure fooled me," Longarm said. "I was just starting to ride around it and look for a way to get in when you opened it up."

"Strangers here generally do," Simpson said with a smile. "I've seen enough to be sure you're who you say you are, so just ride right on in." He gestured toward the gap. "I'll be with you just as soon as I can get inside and close the door."

Longarm toed his horse to start it moving and reined it toward the opening. The animal tossed its head a time or two as it reached the gap in the wall, but moved on through the wide slit. It stopped inside the building when Longarm twitched the reins. He turned in the saddle in time to see Simpson begin cranking a massive wheel that was set on one of the roof's supporting pillars.

As big as was the section of the building's wall, it moved slowly and silently back into place. Longarm could see now that the huge movable portion of the wall traveled on small wheels along an overhead track, much like those which guided the sliding doors of a railroad freight car. At the bottom edge of the door other small wheels that ran in a track set into a groove in the floor both guided and supported much of the wall section's weight.

Longarm did not dismount at once, but sat in his saddle surveying the big oval enclosure. Around the perimeter of the building there were small round-domed furnaces, all of them dark now. Around all the furnaces there were anvils, large cast-iron cauldrons, and frames that supported buckets with long handles as well as sledges and blacksmith's hammers.

Longarm dismounted as the gap in the wall closed. Turning to face the smelter boss, he said, "This is sure some fancy rig-up you got here. I got to admit that it looks like it works pretty good, except that I don't see nobody around to do any kinda work."

"We had to do some work on the doors, so we've been shut down for a few days," Simpson replied. "I've had to turn away a bunch of jobs, but mostly they're from prospectors that we do smelting for regularly."

"And you get strangers dropping in too, I'd imagine?"

"Oh, sure," Simpson said, a smile forming on his face. "They're about like you are about our doors, Marshal Long, but they get used to them after a while."

"Well, it's your new customers I'd like to talk to you

about," Longarm went on. "Have you had some drop in lately?"

"Not as many as I'd like to see, but there's enough on our waiting list right now to keep us busy when we open up again."

"Was there one of 'em that brought you a job that'd be a little bit outside of your regular kind of work?"

"Yes, there was," Simpson said. "One man. How did you happen to know that?"

"I'll get to that in a minute," Longarm promised. "First of all, I'd appreciate you telling me what he looked like."

"Well, he was a big man, and he acted like he was in a pretty big hurry. He said he wanted to get some special work done, something unusual, but he wouldn't tell me what it was after he found out we were shut down temporarily."

"I guess you got a pretty good look at him? Maybe noticed his hands?"

Simpson looked startled. "Now how would you know that? Unless he wasn't some kind of outlaw you're after."

"Never mind that," Longarm answered. "Just tell me what you recall about his hands."

"Why, they were big. And he had some sort of scar on one of them. I couldn't tell what it was from, or much about what it looked like."

"Well, now you've told me just about all I need to know," Longarm said. "Except for one thing. Is he supposed to come back again after you open up?"

"Yes, he is," Simpson said. "But I'd like to know why you're so interested and know so much about this fellow. Are you after him?"

Longarm did not reply for a moment, then he said, "I'd imagine you can keep a tight mouth if I tell you?"

"I can if you want me to."

135

"All right," Longarm said. "I've been chasing after that fellow longer'n I like to think about. He's a killer and a crook from up at Grant's Pass. He's trying to get away with two sacks of double eagles he stole from the U.S. Government."

"You mean to say you've followed him here to Jacksonville?"

"That's the size of it," Longarm replied. "I ain't caught up with him yet, but I don't figure it'll take me long now."

Simpson was silent for a moment, a puzzled frown forming on his face. Then he said, "Maybe I wasn't listening to you carefully enough, Marshal Long, but I'd sure like for you to tell me how the smelter's mixed up in your case."

"Well, a man in my line of work gets sent out on a lot of kinds of cases," Longarm replied. "And all of 'em is a mite different."

"Oh, I can see that," Simpson said. "But what I'm curious to know is how this job has brought you here and what it has to do with the smelter."

"Mostly it was because of what I heard. I stopped for the night at a place along the trail that was run by a fellow who'd grown up here. He told me about your smelter, along with a blacksmith in Butte Falls. Why, I didn't even know there was a smelter still running anyplace close by."

"Sounds to me like that was Mart Edmonds' place you stopped at," Simpson said. "He'd know about the smelter, all right. He was working here even before they tore down the old smelter and built this one. Fine old fellow, Mart is."

"I sure got to agree to that," Longarm said. "Anyway, this outlaw I'm after killed the fellow that he was working for, man that had a bank up north from here, in Grant's Pass. And he stole two sacks of new-minted double eagles. The mint in San Francisco had sent them to the U.S. marshal's office in Grant's Pass."

"Why the devil would they do that?" Simpson asked.

"Oh, that's easy. The mint sends the gold pieces they put out to the U.S. marshal closest to the banks they're intended for," Longarm explained. "And then it's the marshal's job to see that the sacks get delivered to the banks."

"Well, it just seems like to me that it's a plumb crazy way to get the job done, but so do a lot of other things the government does," Simpson said. "So to get back to what's brought you here, you're wondering if I've seen those two sacks of double eagles that somebody stole up north. Am I right?"

"Right as rain," Longarm agreed. "Now, since the sacks were full of brand-new double eagles that ain't been put in circulation yet, it's real likely the crook that stole 'em knew that, because he worked for an even bigger crook in a bank. Anyhow, the fellow that got away with those two sacks of gold pieces was smart enough to know he'd be caught up quick if he tried to spend too many of 'em at one time. So I figured he'd have them melted down and poured into bar-molds."

"Why the devil would he want to do that?" Simpson asked. "He'd be losing money."

"Well, now, I wouldn't exactly say that," Longarm said. "And I'd be right interested in knowing how you figure it."

"I suppose that only a smelter-man would look at it the way I do," Simpson explained. "But any minted gold piece has to have some copper and antimony mixed with it to harden it, keep it from rubbing smooth too soon. Now, a melt-down would get rid of that copper and antimony. The copper'd rise to the surface of the melt and the antimony'd go up in smoke. But the catch is that whoever did the melting would lose the weight that's added to minted gold pieces."

Longarm was silent for a moment. At last he asked, "How much gold would he lose?"

"He wouldn't lose any gold. In fact, the gold he'd have left would be worth a bit more because it'd be about ninety-nine percent pure. But it still wouldn't bring as much as a double eagle. Maybe four or five dollars less."

"If I didn't get mixed up, he'd still come out pretty good," Longarm said. "And he'd be safer if he had a mind to sell that gold in chunks or shavings. He'd still have a right nice-sized amount of pure gold, and there wouldn't be any way to prove that he'd stolen it."

Simpson had listened intently to Longarm. Now he said, "You've got things figured out to a pretty fine point. Would you mind telling if you ever worked in a smelter, Marshal Long?"

"Oh, I worked at a lot of jobs when I was a young fellow trying to find out what I'd like to do best," Longarm replied. "It just happened that one of 'em was in a little smelter back in West Virginia. But I didn't cotton all that much to what I had to do there and I moved on to a different line of work. But I'd heard the smelter-men talk enough to pick up a little bit, and I reckon it's still stuck in my mind."

"I see," Simpson replied. "And the reason why you've come to a smelter starts making sense. But why'd you pick out *this* one?"

"Now, just keep in mind that I didn't pick it out," Longarm said quickly. "All I did was follow that gold thief, and he led me here to Jacksonville."

"Well, if he was leading you, I can guarantee that you did a good job of following him," Simpson said. "And if this fellow we're talking about shows up again, I'd be betting that you'll be waiting here to nab him."

"That's what I got in mind, all right," Longarm said. "But I didn't figure on your smelter being closed down. And chances are that this crook I'm after didn't figure on it either. But what I got to work out is what's going to happen now that he knows he can't get any gold melted here. Is it likely he'll head someplace else before I can catch up with him?"

"If he's looking for a smelter, he'll have a long trip," Simpson said. "And somehow I just can't see him going all the way down to San Francisco to find one. He'd be better off just waiting here until we get into operation again."

"Well, now, that gives me a real good feeling," Longarm told him. "How about over to the east? You'd likely know what's happening in your trade."

"Oh, there's gold mining all along the hills to the southeast, but if the man you're after knows anything about this part of the country he wouldn't be likely to head that way," Simpson said.

"You sound pretty sure about that," Longarm said.

"I am sure, Marshal Long. Now and then I'll have a drifter drop in, some fellow who knows the trade, looking for work. They always like to visit and swap lies a while, so I guess I've got about as good an idea as anybody about what's going on in this business for a pretty good distance in all directions. The nearest smelter in that direction is about a hundred miles away."

Longarm nodded. "What you said is just about what I figured out. And it's good news for me. After what you've said, I'm right sure the fellow I'm after is going to show up here again. Matter of fact, I'd bet dollars to doughnuts that he's in town right now, resting up and waiting."

"And you want me to send word to you when or if he comes here to the smelter?"

"You hit the nail square on the head," Longarm replied. "I don't know whereabouts I'll be stopping, but soon as I've looked around a bit and got me a place to stop, I'll come back out here and tell you where you can find me."

"Try Mrs. Morton's boardinghouse," Simpson suggested. "She doesn't serve meals, but her place is right close to the middle of town, and there's some restaurants handy to it."

"Well, I thank you kindly for the information, and I'll just ride right on back to town and see if I can get settled in. Now, I might not be around the boardinghouse when that crook comes out to see you, but I'll be sure to leave word where I've gone, and I'll get out here quicker'n you can tie up a shoelace."

Chapter 13

Longarm's lengthy visit with Clem Simpson had given his horse the time it needed for a good rest, but though it almost matched its earlier friskiness on the road from the smelter back to Jacksonville, he did not push the animal. Nor did he waste any time, for the sun was far down toward the skyline, and in the east the blue that marked the beginning of night was already beginning to shade the horizon-line.

In his hurry to reach the smelter on his way out of town, Longarm had paid little attention to anything except the road and the odd-looking building which had been his objective. Now he took time to study his surroundings as he let his horse set its own gait. Though an occasional glow brightened a few of the windows in the small clusters of buildings that were visible ahead, he could see nothing moving on the road in front of him; it was completely deserted.

"Old son," he said under his breath, "if you don't get to some kind of eating-place pretty soon, your belly's going to think your throat's been cut."

Soon after he'd passed the first of the shabby houses,

Longarm could see more lights ahead of him. They grew steadily brighter as well as more numerous, and now Longarm could make out a pattern that defined the town. Then, as he rounded one of the sharp curves in the road, a flood of brightness drew his attention to a building set back from the road.

Longarm blinked his eyes a time or two as he moved closer to the building; then his lips curled into a smile when he realized that the burst of light came from a carbide lantern on the roof of the building. The sign bore one word: "Saloon."

"Well, now, old son," he said. "That's something I like. A tot of Tom Moore'd sure be a big help right now. And maybe this place has got some food that'll save you from starving till you can get to town and get a real supper. The only way to find out is to go inside and belly up to the bar."

Suiting action to his words, Longarm reined his horse to the hitch rail and pushed through the saloon's swinging doors. There were no customers in the place, but an aproned barkeep was busy at the end of the long stretch of mahogany, polishing glasses. The man looked up when he saw Longarm enter, finished his work on the glass he was holding, and placed both glass and towel on the bar before moving toward Longarm.

"Evening, friend," he said. "What's your pleasure?"

Longarm nodded a greeting. "Now, I hate to interrupt a man when he's busy like I see you are. But my guzzle's so dry it feels like somebody's been going over it with sandpaper." He was digging into his pocket as he spoke. Taking out a silver dollar, he dropped it to jingle on the bar. "So if you got a bottle of Tom Moore handy, you can just set it out here and I'll pour me a swallow while you get on with your work."

142

"It hurts me when I've got to disappoint a thirsty man, but it just happens I'm out of Tom Moore right now," the barkeep replied. "If you've got a taste for rye, though, I've got some double-aged Old Joe Gideon that oughta satisfy you. It comes out of the same part of Kentucky that Moore does."

"Looks like it'll have to do then," Longarm told him. "And right this minute my guzzle's so full of trail-dust that I'd swallow down a tot of almost anything."

Even before Longarm had finished speaking the barkeeper was turning to the back bar. He picked up a whiskey bottle in one hand and a shotglass in the other, and placed them in front of Longarm. He made no effort to reach for the coin on the bar as his hand brushed over it.

"Just feel free to pour your own," the barkeeper said. He still made no move to pick up the coin. "Or if you'd rather, I'll pour for you."

"Why, I never am too tired to pour myself a drink," Longarm told him.

"You're new in Jacksonville, ain't you?" the barkeeper asked. "At least, I don't recall seeing you here before."

"I reckon you might say I'm just passing through," Longarm answered. He did not look directly at the barkeeper, but had picked up the bottle and was concentrating on filling his glass. As he replaced the bottle on the bar he went on. "But I aim to be around a few days. I've been figuring to meet up with a fellow here in Jacksonville, and so far I ain't seen hide nor hair of him. He might've gone out to the smelter at one time or another, and maybe he stopped off here for a drink."

"If he did, he'd be one of just a few," the barkeeper said. "What's he look like?"

"He's a big man," Longarm answered. "And he's sorta dark-complected. He might have a set of short whiskers.

143

If he was to've stopped off, you'd likely recall seeing that he's got a scar on the back of one hand. It'd remind you a little bit of a fishhook."

"Oh, sure," the barman said. "I do remember a fellow with a mark on his hand. Seems to me he stopped in both ways from the smelter, going out and coming back."

"Riding a roan horse, was he?" Longarm asked, being careful to keep his voice casual. "And he'd be apt to have a led horse that was a dun."

"Now, I can't say as to that. All I know is what I saw when he was inside here."

"How long ago was it that he stopped?"

"Two days ago, maybe three. I just can't recall exactly," the barkeeper replied.

"And you haven't seen him since then?"

"Not hair nor hide. And if he'd've stopped in again, I'm likely to've remembered it, because business hasn't been all that good this last week or so, not since they closed down the smelter to start working on it."

"Well, from what I heard from the boss-man when I was there, it won't be too much longer before it's open again," Longarm said. "But now I'm going to ask you for a favor."

"It won't do any harm for you to ask," the barkeeper said. "But I won't guarantee anything before I hear what it is."

"Oh, I wouldn't ask anything of you that'd get you into trouble," Longarm said. He was slipping his wallet from his pocket as he spoke. He flipped it open and showed his badge and identification to the saloon-keeper. "I'd guess you see why I been asking you so many questions. This fellow I been asking about is a killer and a thief, and I'm trying to find him."

"I always try to go along with the law, Marshal Long," the bartender said. "And I don't have to ask you what

144

you'll want me to do. If this man you're after stops in here again, I'll get word to you right away. Just tell me where you'll be."

"I haven't got a place to stay so far," Longarm replied. "But don't worry about that. There's two easy ways for you to get word to me."

"Maybe you'd better tell me what they are," the barkeep suggested.

"First off, I'll tell whoever's in charge of the local law where I'm going to be if I got to go anyplace. I'll also fix it up with the Beekman Bank to get a message to me."

"You're working for the Beekman brothers then?"

"Not likely. I'm working for Uncle Sam. But there's a fellow in the bank named Forbes, he's one of their big muckety-mucks, and he said the bank would be glad to help if I need any. He'll know where I am."

"I guess that'd be all right," the bartender said. "Like I said, I'm on the side of the law, and I won't forget to do what you asked me to, you can count on that."

"You're sure it won't put you out too much, maybe having to close down while you're in town looking for me?"

"Why, I won't need to close a minute, Marshal Long. Most of the time I'll have a customer or two in here, and I know most of 'em well enough so they'll do me a favor, like looking after the place here while I'm taking word into town for you."

"Then we ain't got too much to worry about," Longarm said. He picked up his glass and downed the last drops it contained before going on. "And now that everything's all straightened out, I better be moseying on, because I got a few little chores to do in town."

In his saddle again, Longarm covered the remaining distance to Jacksonville in a short time. As he entered the town's main street, darkness was almost full, and signs of the day's dying were already beginning to show. In the somewhat dilapidated business buildings lamplights were glowing, and people were still moving along the streets. Reining up in front of the first "Restaurant" sign he saw, Longarm went inside and dropped onto a stool at the counter, which spanned one side of the wall.

"I'll settle for ham and eggs," Longarm told the aproned waiter who came to take his order. "I don't guess it'll take too long to fix 'em up, will it?"

"Just long enough for me to go after 'em," the man replied. "That's one order we always keep ready on the back burner."

Within a very few moments the waiter returned carrying a platter of eggs, ham, and hash-browned potatoes. "You'll likely want coffee, I'd imagine?" he asked as he put the platter down in front of Longarm.

"Oh, sure. And I need to ask you where I need to go to find a marshal or a sheriff, or maybe you got a constable here to keep the law."

"When you step outside, turn right and go on down the street," the waiter replied. "There's a big store down a ways on the right-hand side, that'll be the Emporium. Turn catty-cornered across the street then, and you'll see the firehouse. There's not any way to miss it; there's a big wagon-tire hanging in a cross-tree in front of it. You'll likely find the town constable inside. His name's Lem Wolford."

"Many thanks," Longarm said. "I don't reckon I'll have any trouble."

Longarm made a quick job of clearing his plate, dropped a silver dollar on the counter to pay for his meal, and went outside to the hitch rack. Mounting his horse, he toed it ahead and moved slowly along the rutted street until he saw the wagon-tire alarm that marked the firehouse. He pulled up and looped his horse's reins around the post that supported the wagon tire, then went into the firehouse.

Horses were standing stolidly in narrow stalls on either side of the big wagon with its water tank, hose coil, and pump handles, and though there were no men in sight he could hear voices coming from the back of the building. Squeezing past the pumper, Longarm followed the murmurs to a cubicle of a room where five men were sitting around a battered table with cards in their hands. They were concentrating on their game, and none of them looked up when Longarm stopped in the doorway.

Longarm tapped lightly on the door frame to draw their attention, and when they looked up he said, "I hate to butt in on a friendly game of cards, but I'm looking for your town constable, Lem Wolford. A fellow down the street said I'd likely find him here."

"You found him all right," one of the card-players replied. Though all the men at the table were husky, Wolford was the largest. "And what's your business, stranger?"

"Why, I'm in the same business you are, Constable Wolford," Longarm said. "My name's Long, Custis Long. Deputy U.S. marshal outa the Denver office, and I'm here on a case I'm working."

"You'd be the one they call Longarm?" Wolford asked as he laid his cards facedown on the table.

"Some folks call me that," Longarm replied. "If you'd like to look at my badge . . ."

"Never mind the folderol," Wolford said. "If what you've got to talk to me about is any sorta confidential case, you and me can go outside and talk, but if you don't mind my friends hearing what you got to say, you can tell me about it right here."

"Oh, there's not anything secret about the case I'm on," Longarm said quickly. "When you come right down to brass tacks, the more you and your friends both know about it, the easier it might be for me to run down the crook I'm after."

"Well, if you feel like setting down, there's a chair over yonder in the corner," Wolford suggested.

"Thanks just the same, but I been forking a horse for a good spell," Longarm replied. "My butt's more'n a mite saddle-sprung, so I'll keep standing up."

"These men here are all ones you can trust," Wolford told him. "That long skinny drink of water across from me's Thad Barnes, he's our fire chief. And the one on his right's Clem Hardacre. The one next to me's Sam Colburn, and this one over on my other side here answers to Slim Gosset."

"I'm right glad to make your acquaintance," Longarm said. "I reckon you'll understand why I busted in your game."

"All of us knows that we generally get in a hurry when there's a job to do like putting out fires or chasing after crooks," Wolford said. "So go on and tell us about this case that you're here on."

"Well, now, to cut it short as I can, I'm after a crook and a killer named Wilson. That's all the name I got for him."

"I reckon you can tell us what he looks like?" Wolford asked.

"Oh, sure," Longarm replied. "But there's more to it than I've got to yet."

"Go ahead then," Wolford said. "And this time I'll try not to bust into what you're saying."

Longarm nodded. "Now, the fellow I'm after is named Wilson, but I don't reckon he's using it right now. He managed to get away from Grant's Pass with two bags of double eagles stolen outa the marshal's office. He also killed a banker there."

"Two bags of double eagles? That's one hell of a lot of money for a crook to get away with," Wolford exclaimed. "And the fellow toting it is around here someplace?"

"I got the best reason in the world to figure he's here in town right now," Longarm answered. "I been following him in a big circle all around hell's half-acre. He was heading for the smelter, figuring to get those eagles melted down."

"Now, hold on!" Wolford said. "Why in tunket would he want to melt them eagles down?"

"Because they were from a brand-new run that the mint in San Francisco was sending out. They'd be dead easy to track back to him if he tried to pass too many of 'em."

"And he was going to melt good double eagles?" Wolford's voice still held a hint of incredulity.

"As close as I can figure, that's what brought him here to Jacksonville," Longarm answered. "He'll likely hole up in town and wait for the smelter to start working again. The boss-man out there says it'll only be a day or two before they start up again. Only, I don't aim to let him go free that long. What I need is for you men to wise me up on the lay of the land here in Jacksonville and maybe keep your eyes peeled for him."

"Well, we'll sure be glad to help," Wolford said. "But this ain't all that big of a town, not much to it when you get off of Main Street. You won't have any trouble finding your way around. Now, suppose you tell us what this man you're after looks like."

"He's a big fellow," Longarm answered. "Dark-complected, don't wear a beard or mustache unless he's let one start to sprout while he was on the way here. And one way you can be sure it's him is that he's got an old tattoo that he tried to cut off on the back of his right hand. It looks sorta like a fishhook, and you can't miss it unless he's got gloves on."

"We don't run much to gloves hereabouts," Wolford said. "So if he's wearing some in this kind of weather, he ought to be easy to spot."

"I'll count on you men keeping your eyes peeled then," Longarm said. "Now, I got one more favor to ask. The fellow I talked to out at the smelter said that a good place for me to stay while I'm in town is a boardinghouse run by a lady named Morton. If he was right, I'll need to know where to find it."

"That's easy," Wolford assured him. "And he didn't give you a bum steer, you'll be all right at Miz Morton's. You said you just rode in from the smelter, so all you need to do is turn around and go back the way you came in. Her place is right in town. Just head for the road toward the smelter but don't turn off on it. Push on past it till you come to a corner where there's a building being wrecked out. Rein onto the left-hand side and go about six houses down. You'll see a big white two-story house on your right that needs a new coat of paint. That'll be Miz Morton's boardinghouse."

"You're sure she'll have a room vacant?" Longarm asked.

"Certain-sure," Wolford answered. "I was talking to her yesterday, and she mentioned it. She's a widow-woman; her husband was killed in a smelter accident about three years ago. She runs a nice, clean place, no bedbugs or anything like that. You'll be comfortable there."

"Then I'll just be moving on," Longarm told the group. He turned to face Wolford. "You'll know where to find me should you run across this fellow I'm after. And I'll be prowling around tomorrow, asking questions, so we'll likely run into each other. Now, I'm going to turn in. I put a lot of miles behind me today, and about all I can think of right now is a bed for the night."

• • •

Longarm reined up in front of the big white two-story house that had been described to him. Except for a few gleams of light coming through an oval of frosted glass set into the front door, the house was dark.

"Well, old son," he told himself, "everybody you talked to so far seems to agree about this place, if you got the right house. Maybe you better go up and knock and see for yourself."

Swinging out of his saddle, Longarm made his way to the house and tapped on the glass door-panel. When he'd waited several moments without a response, he tapped again. He'd just dropped his hand when a shadowy form darkened the panel and the door opened a few inches. Now he could see the figure of a woman silhouetted against the dim lamplight glowing from inside.

With the light in his eyes Longarm could make out little but her outline. Before she could speak he said, "I got to ask you to excuse me for bothering you so late, ma'am, but if you're Miz Morton, I'm looking for a room to rent."

"I'm Melinda Morton all right, and I've got a room vacant. But I'd like to know who sent you here before I ask you inside."

"It was Lem Wolford and his friends at the firehouse that told me about you having rooms for rent, Miz Morton. And Mr. Forbes at the bank. But maybe I better tell you who I am. My name's Long, Custis Long. I'm a deputy United States marshal here in Jacksonville on a case."

"That's all I need to ease my mind," she replied, opening the door a bit wider. "Please, come in. It makes a great deal of difference to me when I know how you happened to knock here."

"Before I step inside, ma'am, I guess I better tell you I'll need a place to keep my horse for the night."

"There's a stable at the back of the house," she said. "And a feed trough with some fodder in it. The horse will add a half-dollar to your room rent; that'll be a dollar and a half."

"That'll suit me just fine," Longarm assured her.

"Then lead your horse around the left side of the house," she said. "There's a lantern hanging outside the barn door. And you can come in the back way. I'll open the door for you."

Longarm went to his horse and led it from the street along the side of the house to the barn, which was visible in the small nimbus of light from the town's main street. After lighting the lantern he made a short job of getting his horse unsaddled and leading the tired animal to the feed trough. He picked up his saddlebags and rifle and stepped outside the barn. A trail of light led to an opened door at the rear of the house, and he followed it.

When he reached the door it opened wider. He stepped inside, and as she closed the door Melinda Morton said, "Well, I'm right glad to bid you welcome, Marshal Long."

Chapter 14

Longarm saw Melinda Morton clearly for the first time
as he stopped inside the door. By the light of the lamp
burning on the kitchen table he could see that she was
a tall woman, almost as tall as he was. She was wearing a night robe held together in front by a sash, and
though he could see that she had wide hips and generous
breasts, the robe concealed as much as it revealed about her
figure.

A few wisps of hair visible around the edges of her
mobcap told him that she was a blonde, and the lamplight
revealed her large blue eyes. In the soft glow Longarm
could do no better than to guess that her age was anywhere
from twenty-five to thirty-five. Her chin line was firm, her
lips full, her nostrils flared from an aquiline nose. Her face
was very lightly lined; aside from the small furrow from her
nose to the corners of her lips she had only a few shallow
creases in her brow.

"I didn't ask if you'd had supper, Marshal Long," she
said. "But I've got some food left over from mine, and
there's a pot of coffee on the stove that's still hot."

"I do thank you for offering to feed me, Miz Morton, but I stopped and had a bite a little spell ago. Coffee, now, that's another thing. What I got with my supper wasn't fit to drink, and a cup of real coffee'd sure taste good right now."

"Then sit down, and I'll sip a swallow or two with you," she said, gesturing to the table that stood across the room. "It'll give us a chance to chat for a few minutes, and get better acquainted."

Longarm dropped his gear beside his chair and removed his hat to hang it on the back of the chair before sitting down. He took a cigar and a match from his pocket, but waited to light it while Melinda placed two cups on the table.

"I hope you don't mind me lighting up, Miz Morton?" he asked as he held up the cigar.

"Of course not, Marshal Long. I'm not a smoker myself, but my late husband was. Tobacco smoke doesn't bother me a bit. And even though I'm still called Mrs. Morton, I feel more at home when folks just call me Melinda, or Linda."

"And I answer best to a nickname myself," he told her. "It's Longarm."

"Then that's settled, Longarm. Now go ahead and light your cigar while I pour our coffee."

Longarm lighted his cigar while Melinda filled the cups from the pot on the stove. She sat down opposite him, and after he'd swallowed the first sip of his coffee she said, "I suppose you're chasing after outlaws or bad men of some kind here."

"I'm on the track of one," Longarm told her. "And I got a hunch I'm pretty close to him right now, but I'll know more about it tomorrow or next day."

"I certainly hope you catch him without too much trouble," she said. "And go back to your wife all safe and sound."

"I'll say thank you for your good wishes, Miz Morton—Linda, that is. But I never got around to getting married, so I don't have a wife to go back to. I just make do for myself."

"That's something we have in common then," Linda said. "But I've noticed that people who don't have somebody to lean on seem to be just as happy as the ones who do."

"I won't argue with you about that," Longarm told her. "I heard an old Chinese saying once—or I guess it was—that the ones who travel alone are the quickest ones to make it to where they're going."

"I think the Chinese are right," she said. "Especially after you get used to the idea."

"And while we're talking about traveling, I've been doing my share these last few days, and likely I'll have a lot more to do before I can close this case I'm on. So if you'll just tell me where the room is that I'll be sleeping in, I'll go on and turn in. I got a lot to do tomorrow."

"Of course!" Melinda said. "It's been thoughtless of me to keep you up. Come with me and I'll show you your room, Longarm. It's right past the head of the stairs."

Longarm followed her up the stairway to the upper floor, where Melinda gestured to an open door a few steps along the hall. "I think you'll find it comfortable," she said. "But if you need anything, my room is the last one down. Just tap on the door. I'm used to having roomers who find they need a bar of soap or something like that and knock on my door, whether it's before breakfast or after supper."

"Why, I don't aim to bother you none, Linda. I'll be in bed and asleep in two minutes myself. I'll just say good night and pop into bed. I got to get an early start tomorrow."

Linda nodded and continued down the hall. Longarm stepped inside his room, and found it dark. He flicked a match into flame, saw a lamp on the bureau at the opposite side of the room, and stepped quickly to light it. Then he wasted no time levering out of his boots, hanging his gunbelt on the head of the bedstead, and stripping off his clothes. He bent over the bureau to blow out the lamp, groped his way to the bed, and dropped into it. He stretched and turned for only a moment before he found a comfortable position, then dropped off to sleep.

Longarm had no idea how long he'd been sleeping when the slight click of his door latch brought him awake. In one swift move he raised up in bed and had his Colt in his hand, its muzzle swiveling toward the door.

"Longarm! Please be careful with that gun!" Linda's voice called from the area of the door. "I'd intended to wake you up in a less startling way!"

Longarm let the Colt's muzzle sag as he replied, "If I'd known it was you coming in, I sure wouldn't've reached for it. But you sure surprised me."

Linda had been moving toward the bed while Longarm was speaking, and now he could make out the shimmering outline of her body, a ghostlike blur in the darkness. As she moved closer and his vision adjusted to the darkness, he could see the darker circles of her full budded breasts and the vee of her pubic brush. Then she reached the bed and sat down beside him.

She said, "I hope you don't mind me coming to visit you, though I'm sure you know why I have."

"Why, Linda, anybody can figure out what a lonesome lady's got in mind when she comes into a man's room at night. But I'm glad you did and you're welcome as the flowers in May. I got to say I'm surprised, though."

"I couldn't sleep for wondering how you'd be as a lover, Longarm. And it didn't take me long to decide to find out."

156

While she spoke, Linda was rubbing her hands over Longarm's muscular chest and biceps. Her hands moved steadily down his body to his crotch. He was still flaccid, though beginning to swell. Linda bent forward until she could engulf him, and the gentle rasping of her agile tongue quickly brought him to a full erection.

Longarm lay back and enjoyed her caresses until the quivers that began to sweep through Linda's body warned him that she was dangerously near to approaching her peak. He lifted her gently then, and Linda helped him as he turned her to lie on her back in the bed. Longarm lost no time kneeling above her, and she spread her thighs while waiting for him to position himself before guiding his erection.

Then Longarm plunged. He drove into the moist depths of her quivering body with a half-dozen lusty drives that brought soft sighing gasps of ecstasy from her lips. Linda squirmed and locked her legs around Longarm's hips, trying to pull him into her even more deeply. Her soft sighs quickly became gasps, and Longarm drove again and again until her gasps grew into small happy moans.

Now Longarm speeded up his thrusts and held himself buried deeply for a few moments between his spells of deep fast driving. When he felt a sudden ripple of frantic movements as Linda began to tremble, he lunged with stronger and more forceful thrusts as he sought his own climax. Then Linda cried out, a light scream that became pulsating throbs as her hips squirmed and rocked and her body trembled, while Longarm reached his own peak with a last lusty drive and held himself pressed to her.

For several minutes neither Linda nor Longarm moved or spoke. At last she said, "Being in bed with a man's nothing new to me, Longarm. I guess you understood that right after we got started. But I'll say this. You're the most man I've ever been to bed with, and if you don't do it again at least twice more before daylight, I'll never get over being disappointed."

"Well, I always try to please a lady," he replied. "And I sure don't aim to stop trying now. So let's just rest a bit, and then we'll get started all over again."

"You know, Lem, after waiting here all the time that I have, two whole days now, I'm just about to figure I've got off that Wilson scoundrel's trail," Longarm said.

He and Lem Wolford were sitting at the scarred and creaky table in the back room of the fire station relaxing after having their noonday meal together.

Wolford replied, "Maybe you're right. But there's just as much chance that your man's holed up somewheres close by, looking for some smoke to come out of the smelter."

"Oh, I've had that idea myself," Longarm told him. "But now that you've fixed up with every lawman in these parts to help look for him, don't you figure somebody'd stumble over him?"

"Seems like they ought've," Wolford agreed. "But don't get all nerved up too fast, Longarm. The smelter just started to put out smoke yesterday. It won't get to letting off no heavy smoke for another day or two."

"Well, I might be nerved up a mite, but I'm sure not giving up," Longarm said. "Was I to . . ."

Longarm broke off as a neatly dressed youth came into the little cubicle. He glanced at Longarm and Wolford, then asked, "Is one of you gentleman U.S. Marshal Long?"

"That's me," Longarm replied.

"I have a message for you from Mr. Forbes at the Beekman Bank," the young man said. As he spoke he was taking an envelope from his inside coat pocket. He handed it over to Longarm and started to leave.

"Hold on!" Longarm said. "I might want to send your Mr. Forbes an answer."

Longarm tore the end off the envelope and slid out a folded half-sheet of paper. Unfolding it, he read the message in neat script: *"Man came into bank asking about spot gold price. Am sure he is the one you inquired about. Unable to follow him, but obvious where he must be heading. Forbes."*

"Well, glory be!" Longarm exclaimed. He turned to the young messenger. "You tell Mr. Forbes I was sure glad to hear from him and that I thank him a lot. Oh, yes, you might say I'll be in later on to tell him so to his face."

"Very good, sir. Thank you," the youth replied. He turned and left as Longarm refolded the note and slid it into his pocket.

"From what you said, that note's good news," Wolford said. "I guess your man's come out of whatever hole he was in?"

"He sure as hell has," Longarm replied. "So I'll be riding out right now, Lem. And I'd be real grateful if you feel like following up on me after I leave."

"Sure, Longarm. I'll be glad to. Even if my badge won't be any good outside of town here, I don't know of any law that says I can't ride a ways after a friend."

"That's about how I figured," Longarm told him. "But now I got the edge, I aim to keep it. That gold Wilson's got makes a real heavy load for a packhorse, so we ought not to have much trouble catching up with him."

Longarm had already started for the door. Once outside, he mounted and reined his horse ahead. Wolford was only a few moments behind him, and within a very few minutes they had left Jacksonville behind and were pushing their horses to a distance-eating canter on the road that led to the smelter.

By the best calculation Longarm could make, Wilson must be ahead of them by at least three quarters of an hour, perhaps longer. Because the road meandered a bit between the low hillocks that rose occasionally, Longarm did not expect to catch sight of his quarry for quite a while. However, he kept his horse moving steadily at a pace that would not overtire the animal, and stood up in his stirrups now and again to get a better view of the terrain ahead.

As he reached the saloon Longarm almost rode past it; then on second thought he waved to Wolford, reined in at the graveled stretch, and rode up to the building's door. The man who'd served him on his earlier visit was rearranging the glasses and bottles on the back bar. He turned when Longarm's boots thunked on the floor and smiled when he recognized Longarm.

"Well!" he said. "You have come for a drink again. I have no Tom Moore yet, but—"

"Never mind Tom Moore or Joe Gideon either," Longarm said. "I'm wondering if you've seen that fellow I asked you about passing by here lately."

"How could you know that?" the barkeep asked. "He did not pass by, but came in for a drink. And you would not believe it, but he paid me with a double eagle and did not ask for change."

"How long ago?"

"A half hour, or a bit less. I was getting ready to send a message to you."

"Thanks for the information," Longarm said. "If luck's riding with us, me and my friend that's outside will be stopping by a little later, and then you can pour some drinks for us both."

Without waiting for the saloon-keeper to reply, Longarm turned and pushed hurriedly through the batwings. Wolford was just reining off the road. He pulled up beside Longarm and said, "This is sure one hell of a time to stop for a drink, Long! We're giving that outlaw the edge!"

"Maybe a mite of one," Longarm replied. He was swinging into his saddle, and as he wheeled his horse around he went on. "Dammit, Lem, you oughta know I ain't fool enough to stop for a drink at a time like this! I wanted to find out for sure that Wilson's still ahead of us. He is, all right, and he ain't got more'n a half-hour lead. It's time for us to spur up and catch him!"

Longarm dug his heels into his mount's flank, and the horse responded in spite of its lathered muzzle and heaving ribs. Wolford wheeled to follow him; he and Longarm reached the road at almost the same moment. They began to drum their heels on the horses' sides and the tiring animals responded by speeding up.

Although to both Longarm and his companion a long stretch of time seemed to pass before they caught sight of Wilson and his led horse, the distance between them and their quarry was not all that great. For several minutes after Longarm and Wolford began closing in on him, the outlaw was not aware that he was being pursued. Then Longarm caught a momentary glimpse of Wilson's face as the outlaw turned to look behind him.

"He's the one we're after all right!" Longarm called to Wolford after his brief look at the man ahead of them. "It's that outlaw Wilson, so we got a real race on our hands now. Trouble is, he's spotted us, but we still got the edge, because he sure can't make much better time with that loaded-down packhorse!"

"We can't go much faster, any more than he can!" Wolford shouted back. "This poor old nag I'm forking is just about foundering right now."

"Mine's still moving pretty good," Longarm replied. "And sooner or later that bastard'll have to make up his mind to let go of the nag that's carrying the gold. That's what we got to look out for, because if he cuts loose he'll likely be able to outrun us!"

When Longarm turned back to scan the road ahead, Wilson and the led horse had vanished. For a moment Longarm felt sure that his eyes were deceiving him; then he risked standing up in his stirrups without trying to check his horse's headlong pace. Ahead he saw that the road curved, and as he turned his head to scan the almost barren landscape, he got a fleeting glimpse of the bobbing tip of Wilson's hat at an angle to his left.

Dropping back in his saddle he turned and called to Wolford. "You keep to the road! I'm going to cut catty-cornered!"

"Hold up, Longarm!" Wolford shouted. "That's a sink where you'll get bogged down!"

Longarm heard his companion's words, but did not try to reply; he was already wheeling his horse at an angle to the road. For a short distance ahead the ground was bare and had a gentle downward slant. Then he saw a sea of gray-green and realized that he was heading for a monstrously broad expanse of chamisal, the close-growing scrub brush that defied penetration by both humans and horses.

Realizing at once that he had no other choice, Longarm reined away from the brushy growth and drummed his heels on his mount's sides, trying to urge it to an even faster gait. The tiring horse responded, and he rode in a course paralleling the edge of the tangled mass of chamisal.

After he'd covered what seemed to be a very long stretch, the chamisal thinned, and across the expanse of barren ground Longarm once more got a glimpse of Wilson and his led horse. This time the outlaw was within rifle range, but only his head and neck were visible above the diminishing patches of the gray-green growth. Longarm reined in and slid his Winchester from its saddle scabbard. He squirmed for a moment to be sure he was firmly seated, then shouldered the rifle and got Wilson in his sights.

There were a few thinning stands of gray-green growth between him and the fleeing outlaw, and the chamisal grew high enough to deflect a bullet. Longarm had learned the virtue of patience. He waited, swinging the barrel of his Winchester to keep his sights fixed on Wilson's head. Then the chamisal gave way to barren soil.

Longarm lowered the muzzle of his rifle a bit and continued to wait patiently. Only when he could see Wilson's shoulders and torso above a stretch of barren ground did he raise the rifle and take aim. He squeezed off a shot. Wilson's shoulders jerked as the rifle's slug went home. His body twisted in the saddle and his arms drooped, letting the reins fall free.

Without guidance or control the horse the outlaw was forking stopped, and the packhorse with its load of gold sacks stopped as well. Wilson toppled to the ground and lay still.

Longarm lowered his Winchester. "Old son," he said into the silent air, "it ain't real often that you luck out this way, but it sure looks like this case you been put on can be closed about now. And that long train ride back to Denver is going to be about the best one you've taken in a long, long time."

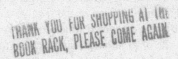

THANK YOU FOR SHOPPING AT THE BOOK RACK, PLEASE COME AGAIN

Watch for

LONGARM AND THE FOOL KILLER

167th in the bold LONGARM series from Jove

Coming in November!

SPECIAL PREVIEW!

Giles Tippette, America's new star of the classic western, tells the epic story of Justa Williams and his family's struggle for survival . . .

Gunpoint

By the acclaimed author of *Sixkiller*, *Hard Rock* and *Jailbreak*.

Here is a special excerpt from this riveting new novel—available from Jove Books . . .

I was standing in front of my house, yawning, when the messenger from the telegraph office rode up. It was a fine, early summer day and I knew the boy, Joshua, from a thousand other telegrams he'd delivered from Blessing, the nearest town to our ranch some seven miles away.

Only this time he didn't hand me a telegram but a hand-written note on cheap foolscap paper. I opened it. It said, in block letters:

I WILL KILL YOU ON SIGHT JUSTA WILLIAMS

Joshua was about to ride away on his mule. I stopped him. I said, "Who gave you this?" gesturing with the note.

He said, "Jus' a white gennelman's thar in town. Give me a dollar to brang it out to you."

"What did he look like?"

He kind of rolled his eyes. "I never taken no notice, Mistuh Justa. I jest done what the dollar tol' me to do."

"Was he old, was he young? Was he tall? Fat?"

"Suh, I never taken no notice. I's down at the train depot

169

an' he came up an ast me could I git a message to you. I said, 'Shorely.' An' then he give me the dollar 'n I got on my mule an' lit out. Did I do wrong?"

"No," I said slowly. I gave his mule a slap on the rump. "You get on back to town and don't say nothing about this. You understand? Not to anybody."

"Yes, suh," he said. And then he was gone, loping away on the good saddle mule he had.

I walked slowly back into my house, looking at the message and thinking. The house was empty. My bride, Nora, and our eight-month-old son had gone to Houston with the balance of her family for a reunion. I couldn't go because I was Justa Williams and I was the boss of the Half-Moon ranch, a spread of some thirty thousand deeded acres and some two hundred thousand other acres of government grazing land. I was going on for thirty years old and I'd been running the ranch since I was about eighteen when my father, Howard, had gone down through the death of my mother and a bullet through the lungs. I had two brothers, Ben, who was as wild as a March hare, and Norris, the middle brother, who'd read too many books.

For myself I was tired as hell and needed, badly, to get away from it all, even if it was just to go on a two-week drunk. We were a big organization. What with the ranch and other property and investments our outfit was worth something like two million dollars. And as near as I could figure, I'd been carrying all that load for all those years without much of a break of any kind except for a week's honeymoon with Nora. In short I was tired and I was given out and I was wishing for a relief from all the damn responsibility. If it hadn't been work, it had been a fight or trouble of some kind. Back East, in that year of 1895, the world was starting to get sort of civilized. But along the coastal bend of Texas, in Matagorda County, a man could still get messages from some nameless person threatening to kill him on sight.

I went on into the house and sat down. It was cool in there, a relief from the July heat. It was a long, low, Mexican ranch-style house with red tile on the roof, a fairly big house with thick walls that Nora had mostly designed. The house I'd grown up in, the big house, the house we called ranch headquarters, was about a half a mile away. Both of my brothers still lived there with our dad and a few cooks and maids of all kinds. But I was tired of work, tired of all of it, tired of listening to folks whining and complaining and expecting me to make it all right. Whatever it was.

And now this message had come. Well, it wasn't any surprise. I'd been threatened before so they weren't getting a man who'd come late in life to being a cherry. I was so damned tired that for a while I just sat there with the message in my hand without much curiosity as to who had sent it.

Lord, the place was quiet. Without Nora's presence and that of my eight-month-old heir, who was generally screaming his head off, the place seemed like it had gone vacant.

For a long time I just sat there, staring at the brief message. I had enemies aplenty but, for the life of me, I couldn't think of any who would send me such a note. Most of them would have came busting through the front door with a shotgun or a pair of revolvers. No, it had to be the work of a gun hired by someone who'd thought I'd done him dirt. And he had to be someone who figured to cause me a good deal of worry in addition to whatever else he had planned for me. It was noontime, but I didn't feel much like eating even though Nora had left Juanita, our cook and maid and maybe the fattest cook and maid in the county, to look after me. She came in and asked me in Spanish what I wanted to eat. I told her nothing and, since she looked so disappointed, I told her she could peel me an apple and fetch it to me. Then I got up and went in my office, where my whiskey was, and poured myself out a good, stiff drink. Most folks would have said it was too hot for hard liquor, but I was not of that mind. Besides, I was mighty glum. Nora hadn't been gone quite a week out of the month's visit she had planned, and already I was mooning around the house and cussing myself for ever giving her permission to go in the first place. That week had given me some idea of how she'd felt when I'd been called away on ranch business of some kind or another and been gone for a considerable time. I'd always thought her complaints had just come from an overwrought female, but I reckoned it had even been lonelier for her. At least now I had my work and was out and about the ranch, while she'd mostly been stuck in the house without a female neighbor nearer than five miles to visit and gossip with.

Of course I could have gone and stayed in the big house; returned to my old ways just as if I were still single. But I was reluctant to do that. For one thing it would have meant eating Buttercup's cooking, which was a chore any sane man would have avoided. But it was considerably more than that; I'd moved out and I had a home and I figured that was the place for me to be. Nora's presence was still there; I could feel it. I could even imagine I could smell the last lingering wisps from her perfume.

Besides that, I figured one or both of my brothers would have some crack to make about not being able to stand my own company or was I homesick for Mommy to come back. We knew each other like we knew our own guns and nothing was off-limits as far as the joshing went.

But I did want to confer with them about the threatening note. That was family as well as ranch business. There was nobody, neither of my brothers, even with Dad's advice, who was capable of running the ranch, which was the cornerstone of our business. If something were to happen to me we would be in a pretty pickle. Many years before I'd started an upgrading program in our cattle by bringing in Shorthorn cattle from the Midwest, Herefords, whiteface purebreds, to breed to our all-bone, horse-killing, half-crazy-half-wild herd of Longhorns. It had worked so successfully that we now had a purebred herd of our own of Herefords, some five hundred of them, as well as a herd of some five thousand crossbreds that could be handled and worked without wearing out three horses before the noon meal. Which had been the case when I'd inherited herds of pure Longhorns when Howard had turned the ranch over to me.

But there was an art in that crossbreeding and I was the only one who really understood it. You just didn't throw a purebred Hereford bull in with a bunch of crossbred cows and let him do the deciding. No, you had to keep herd books and watch your bloodlines and breed for a certain conformation that would give you the most beef per pound of cow. As a result, our breeding program had produced cattle that we easily sold to the Northern markets for nearly twice what my stubborn neighbors were getting for their cattle.

I figured to go over to the big house and show the note to my brothers and Howard and see what they thought, but I didn't figure to go until after supper. It had always been our custom, even after my marriage, for all of us to gather in the big room that was about half office and half sitting room and sit around discussing the day's events and having a few after-supper drinks. It was also then when, if anybody had any proposals, they could present them to me for my approval. Norris ran the business end of our affairs, but he couldn't make a deal over a thousand dollars without my say-so. Of course that was generally just a formality since his was the better judgment in such matters. But there had to be just one boss and that was me. As I say, a situation I was finding more and more wearisome.

I thought to go up to the house about seven of the evening. Juanita would have fixed my supper and they would have had theirs, and we'd all be relaxed and I could show them the note and get their opinion. Personally, I thought it was somebody's idea of a prank. If you are going to kill a man it ain't real good policy to warn him in advance.

About seven I set out walking toward the big house. It was just coming dusk and there was a nice breeze blowing in from the gulf. I kept three saddle horses in the little corral behind my house, but I could walk the half mile in just about the same time as it would take me to get up a horse and get him saddled and bridled. Besides, the evening was pleasant and I felt the need to stretch my legs.

I let myself into the house through the back door, passed the door to the dining room, and then turned left into the big office. Dad was sitting in his rocking chair near to the door of the little bedroom he occupied. Norris was working at some papers on his side of the big double desk we shared. Ben was in a straight-backed chair he had tilted back against the wall. The whiskey was on the table next to Ben. When I came in the room he said, "Well, well, if it ain't the deserted bridegroom. Taken to loping your mule yet?"

I made a motion as if to kick the chair out from under him and said, "Shut up, Ben. You'd be the one to know about that."

Howard said, "Any word from Nora yet, son?"

I shook my head. "Naw. I told her to go and enjoy herself and not worry about writing me." I poured myself out a drink and then went and sat in a big easy chair that was

174

against the back wall. Norris looked up from his work and said, "Justa, how much higher are you going to let this cattle market go before you sell off some beef?"

"About a week," I said. "Maybe a little longer."

"Isn't that sort of taking a gamble? The bottom could fall out of this market any day."

"Norris, didn't anybody ever tell you that ranching was a gamble?"

"Yes," he said, "I believe you've mentioned that three or four hundred times. But the point is I could use the cash right now. There's a new issue of U.S. treasury bonds that are paying four percent. Those cattle we should be shipping right now are about to reach the point of diminishing returns."

Ben said, "Whatever in the hell that means."

I said, "I'll think it over." I ragged Norris a good deal and got him angry at every good opportunity, but I generally listened when he was talking about money.

After that Ben and I talked about getting some fresh blood in the horse herd. The hard work was done for the year but some of our mounts were getting on and we'd been crossbreeding within the herd too long. I told Ben I thought he ought to think about getting a few good Morgan studs and breeding them in with some of our younger quarter-horse mares. For staying power there was nothing like a Morgan. And if you crossed that with the quick speed of a quarter horse you had something that would stay with you all day under just about any kind of conditions.

After that we talked about this and that, until I finally dragged the note out of my pocket. I said, not wanting to make it seem too important, "Got a little love letter this noon. Wondered what ya'll thought about it." I got out of my chair and walked over and handed it to Ben. He read it and then brought all four legs of his chair to the floor with a thump and read it again. He looked over at me. "What the hell! You figure this to be the genuine article?"

I shrugged and went back to my chair. "I don't know," I said. "I wanted to get ya'll's opinion."

Ben got up and handed the note to Norris. He read it and then raised his eyebrows. "How'd you get this?"

"That messenger boy from the telegraph office, Joshua, brought it out to me. Said some man had given him a dollar to bring it out."

"Did you ask him what the man looked like?"

I said drily, "Yes, Norris, I asked him what the man looked like but he said he didn't know. Said all he saw was the dollar."

Norris said, "Well, if it's somebody's idea of a joke it's a damn poor one." He reached back and handed the letter to Howard.

Dad was a little time in reading the note since Norris had to go and fetch his spectacles out of his bedroom. When he'd got them adjusted he read it over several times and then looked at me. "Son, I don't believe this is something you can laugh off. You and this ranch have made considerable enemies through the years. The kind of enemies who don't care if they were right or wrong and the kind of enemies who carry a grudge forever."

"Then why warn me?"

Norris said, "To get more satisfaction out of it. To scare you."

I looked at Dad. He shook his head. "If they know Justa well enough to want to kill him they'll also know he don't scare. No, there's another reason. They must know Justa ain't all that easy to kill. About like trying to corner a cat in a railroad roundhouse. But if you put a man on his guard and keep him on his guard, it's got to eventually take off

176

some of the edge. Wear him down to where he ain't really himself. The same way you buck down a bronc. Let him do all the work against himself."

I said, "So you take it serious, Howard?"

"Yes, sir," he said. "I damn well do. This ain't no prank."

"What shall I do?"

Norris said, "Maybe we ought to run over in our minds the people you've had trouble with in the past who've lived to bear a grudge."

I said, "That's a lot of folks."

Ben said, "Well, there was that little war we had with that Preston family over control of the island."

Howard said, "Yes, but that was one ranch against another."

Norris said, "Yes, but they well knew that Justa was running matters, as does everyone who knows this ranch. So any grudge directed at the ranch is going to be directed right at Justa."

I said, with just a hint of bitterness, "Was that supposed to go with the job, Howard? You didn't explain that part to me."

Ben said, "What about the man in the buggy? He sounds like a likely suspect for such a turn."

Norris said, "But he was crippled."

Ben gave him a sour look. "He's from the border, Norris. You reckon he couldn't hire some gun help?"

Howard said, "Was that the hombre that tried to drive that herd of cattle with tick fever through our range? Those Mexican cattle that hadn't been quarantined?"

Norris said, "Yes, Dad. And Justa made that little man, whatever his name was, drive up here and pay damages."

Ben said, "And he swore right then and there that *he'd* make Justa pay damages."

I said, "For my money it's got something to do with that

177

maniac up in Bandera County that kept me locked up in a root cellar for nearly a week and then tried to have me hung for a crime I didn't even know about."

"But you killed him. And damn near every gun hand he had."

I said, "Yeah, but there's always that daughter of his. And there was a son."

Ben gave me a slight smile. "I thought ya'll was close. I mean *real* close. You and the daughter."

I said, "What we done didn't have anything to do with anything. And I think she was about as crazy as her father. And Ben, if you ever mention that woman around Nora, I'm liable to send you one of those notes."

Norris said, "But that's been almost three years ago."

I shook my head. "Time ain't nothing to a woman. They got the patience of an Indian. She'd wait this long just figuring it'd take that much time to forget her."

Norris said skeptically, "That note doesn't look made by a woman's hand."

I said, "It's block lettering, Norris. That doesn't tell you a damn thing. Besides, maybe she hired a gun hand who could write."

Ben said, "I never heard of one."

Howard said, waving the note, "Son, what are you going to do about this?"

I shrugged. "Well, Dad, I don't see where there's anything for me to do right now. I can't shoot a message and until somebody either gets in front of me or behind me or *somewheres,* I don't see what I can do except keep a sharp lookout."

The next day I was about two miles from ranch headquarters, riding my three-year-old bay gelding down the little wagon track that led to Blessing, when I heard the

178

whine of a bullet passing just over my head, closely followed by the crack of a distant rifle. I never hesitated; I just fell off my horse to the side away from the sound of the rifle. I landed on all fours in the roadbed, and then crawled as quick as I could toward the sound and into the high grass. My horse had run off a little ways, surprised at my unusual dismount. He turned his head to look at me, wondering, I expected, what the hell was going on.

But I was too busy burrowing into that high grass as slow as I could so as not to cause it to ripple or sway or give away my position in any other way to worry about my horse. I took off my hat on account of its high crown, and then I eased my revolver out of its holster, cocking it as I did. I was carrying a .42/.40 Navy Colt, which is a .40-caliber cartridge chamber on a .42-caliber frame. The .42-caliber frame gave it a good weight in the hand with less barrel deviation, and the .40-caliber bullets it fired would stop anything you hit in the right place. But it still wasn't any match for a rifle at long range, even with the six-inch barrel. My enemy, whoever he was, could just sit there patiently and fire at the slightest movement, and he had to eventually get me because I couldn't lay out there all day. It was only ten of the morning, but already the sun was way up and plenty hot. I could feel a little trickle of sweat running down my nose, but I dare not move to wipe it away for fear even that slight movement could be seen. And I couldn't chance raising my head enough to see for that too would expose my position. All I could do was lay there, staring down at the earth, and wait, knowing that at any second, my bushwhacker could be making his way silently in my direction. He'd have to know, given the terrain, the general location of where I was hiding.

Of course he might have thought he'd hit me, especially from the way I'd just fallen off my horse. I took a cautious look to my left. My horse was still about ten yards away, cropping at the grass along the side of the road. Fortunately, the tied reins had fallen behind the saddle horn and were held there. If I wanted to make a run for it I wouldn't have to spend the time gathering up the reins. The bad part of that was that our horses were taught to ground-rein. When you got off, if you dropped the reins they'd stand there just as if they were tied to a stump. But this way my horse was free to wander off as the spirit might move him. Leaving me afoot whilst being stalked by a man with a rifle.

I tried to remember how close the bullet had sounded over my head and whether or not the assassin might have thought he'd hit me. He had to have been firing upward because there was no other concealment except the high grass. Then I got to thinking I hadn't seen a horse. Well, there were enough little depressions in the prairie that he could have hid a horse some ways back and then come forward on foot and concealed himself in the high grass when he saw me coming.

But how could he have known I was coming? Well, that one wasn't too hard to figure out. I usually went to town at least two or three times a week. If the man had been watching me at all he'd of known that. So then all he'd of had to do was come out every morning and just wait. Sooner or later he was bound to see me coming along, either going or returning.

But I kept thinking about that shot. I'd had my horse in a walk, just slouching along. And God knows, I made a big enough target. In that high grass he could easily have concealed himself close enough for an easy shot, especially if he was a gun hand. The more I thought about it the more I began to think the shooter had been aiming to miss me, to scare me, to wear me down as Howard had said. If the note had come from somebody with an old grudge, they'd *want* me to know who was about to kill me or have me killed. And a bushwhacking rifle shot wasn't all that personal. Maybe the idea was to just keep worrying me until I got to twitching and where I was about a quarter of a second slow. That would be about all the edge a good gun hand would need.

I'd been laying there for what I judged to be a good half hour. Unfortunately I'd crawled in near an ant mound and there was a constant stream of the little insects passing by my hands. Sooner or later one of them was going to sting me. By now I was soaked in sweat and starting to get little cramps from laying so still. I know I couldn't stay there much longer. At any second my horse might take it into his head to go loping back to the barn. As it was he was steadily eating his way further and further from my position.

I made up my mind I was going to have to do something. I cautiously and slowly raised my head until I could just see over the grass. There wasn't anything to see except grass. There was no man, no movement, not even a head of cattle that the gunman might have secreted himself behind.

I took a deep breath and moved, jamming my hat on my head as I did and ramming my gun into its holster. I ran, keeping as low as I could, to my horse. He gave me a startled look, but he didn't spook. Ben trains our horses to expect nearly anything. If they are of a nervous nature we don't keep them.

I reached his left side, stuck my left boot in the stirrup, and swung my right leg just over the saddle. Then, hanging on to his side, I grabbed his right rein with my right hand and pulled his head around until he was pointing up the road. I was holding onto the saddle with my left hand. I kicked him in the ribs as best I could, and got him into a trot and then into a lope going up the road toward town. I tell you, it was hell hanging on to his side. I'd been going a-horseback since I could walk, but I wasn't no trick rider and the position I was in made my horse run sort of sideways so that his gait was rough and awkward.

But I hung on him like that for what I judged to be a quarter of a mile and out of rifle shot. Only then did I pull myself up into the saddle and settle myself into a normal position to ride a horse. Almost immediately I pulled up and turned in the saddle to look back. Not a thing was stirring, just innocent grass waving slightly in the light breeze that had sprung up.

I shook my head, puzzled. Somebody was up to something, but I was damned if I could tell what. If they were trying to make me uneasy they were doing a good job of it. And the fact that I was married and had a wife and child to care for, and a hell of a lot more reason to live than when I was a single man, was a mighty big influence in my worry. It could be that the person behind the threats was aware of that and was taking advantage of it. If such was the case, it made me think more and more that it was the work of the daughter of the maniac in Bandera that had tried in several ways to end my life. It was the way a woman would think because she would know about such things. I couldn't visualize the man in the buggy understanding that a man with loved ones will cling harder to life for their sake than a man with nothing else to lose except his own hide.

LONGARM

Explore the exciting Old West with
one of the men who made it wild!

___LONGARM AND THE LONE STAR CAPTIVE   0-515-10646-1/$4.50
  (Giant novel)
___LONGARM AND THE GOLD HUNTERS #153   0-515-10669-0/$3.50
___LONGARM AND THE COLORADO   0-515-10689-5/$3.50
  GUNDOWN #154
___LONGARM AND THE GRAVE ROBBERS #155   0-515-10708-5/$3.50
___LONGARM AND THE ARKANSAS AMBUSH   0-515-10733-6/$3.50
  #156
___LONGARM AND THE ARIZONA SHOWDOWN   0-515-10753-0/$3.50
  #157
___LONGARM AND THE UTE NATION #158   0-515-10790-5/$3.50
___LONGARM IN THE SIERRA ORIENTAL #159   0-515-10808-1/$3.50
___LONGARM AND THE GUNSLICKS #160   0-515-10832-4/$3.50
___LONGARM AND THE LADY SHERIFF #161   0-515-10849-9/$3.50
___LONGARM ON THE DEVIL'S HIGHWAY #162   0-515-10865-0/$3.50
___LONGARM AND THE CIMARRON CITY   0-515-10880-4/$3.50
  SELLOUT #163
___LONGARM AND THE CHEYENNE KID #164   0-515-10901-0/$3.99
___LONGARM AND THE REBEL BRAND #165   0-515-10929-0/$3.99
___LONGARM AND THE DOUBLE EAGLES #165   0-515-10955-X/$3.99
___LONGARM AND THE FOOL KILLER #167   0-515-10980-0/$3.99
  (Nov. 1992)
___LONGARM AND THE SHOSHONI SILVER #168   0-515-10997-5/$3.99
  (Dec. 1992)

For Visa, MasterCard and American Express orders ($15 minimum) call: 1-800-631-8571

FOR MAIL ORDERS: CHECK BOOK(S). FILL OUT COUPON. SEND TO:	POSTAGE AND HANDLING: $1.75 for one book, 75¢ for each additional. Do not exceed $5.50.
BERKLEY PUBLISHING GROUP 390 Murray Hill Pkwy., Dept. B East Rutherford, NJ 07073	BOOK TOTAL $ _____
	POSTAGE & HANDLING $ _____
NAME_____	APPLICABLE SALES TAX $ _____
ADDRESS_____	(CA, NJ, NY, PA)
CITY_____	TOTAL AMOUNT DUE $ _____
STATE _____ ZIP _____	PAYABLE IN US FUNDS.
PLEASE ALLOW 6 WEEKS FOR DELIVERY. PRICES ARE SUBJECT TO CHANGE WITHOUT NOTICE.	(No cash orders accepted.) 201e

If you enjoyed this book, subscribe now and get...

TWO FREE

A $7.00 VALUE–

If you would like to read more of the very best, most exciting, adventurous, action-packed Westerns being published today, you'll want to subscribe to True Value's Western Home Subscription Service.

Each month the editors of True Value will select the 6 very best Westerns from America's leading publishers for special readers like you. You'll be able to preview these new titles as soon as they are published, *FREE* for ten days with no obligation!

TWO FREE BOOKS

When you subscribe, we'll send you your first month's shipment of the newest and best 6 Westerns for you to preview. With your first shipment, two of these books will be yours as our introductory gift to you absolutely *FREE* (a $7.00 value), regardless of what you decide to do. If you like them, as much as we think you will, keep all six books but pay for just 4 at the low subscriber rate of just $2.75 each. If you decide to return them, keep 2 of the titles as our gift. No obligation.

Special Subscriber Savings

When you become a True Value subscriber you'll save money several ways. First, all regular monthly selections will be billed at the low subscriber price of just $2.75 each. That's at least a savings of $4.50 each month below the publishers price. Second, there is never any shipping, handling or other hidden charges—*Free home delivery*. What's more there is no minimum number of books you must buy, you may return any selection for full credit and you can cancel your subscription at any time. A TRUE VALUE!

A special offer for people who enjoy reading the best Westerns published today.

WESTERNS!

NO OBLIGATION

Mail the coupon below

To start your subscription and receive 2 FREE WESTERNS, fill out the coupon below and mail it today. We'll send your first shipment which includes 2 FREE BOOKS as soon as we receive it.

Mail To: **True Value Home Subscription Services, Inc. P.O. Box 5235
120 Brighton Road, Clifton, New Jersey 07015-5235**

YES! I want to start reviewing the very best Westerns being published today. Send me my first shipment of 6 Westerns for me to preview FREE for 10 days. If I decide to keep them, I'll pay for just 4 of the books at the low subscriber price of $2.75 each; a total $11.00 (a $21.00 value). Then each month I'll receive the 6 newest and best Westerns to preview Free for 10 days. If I'm not satisfied I may return them within 10 days and owe nothing. Otherwise I'll be billed at the special low subscriber rate of $2.75 each; a total of $16.50 (at least a $21.00 value) and save $4.50 off the publishers price. There are never any shipping, handling or other hidden charges. I understand I am under no obligation to purchase any number of books and I can cancel my subscription at any time, no questions asked. In any case the 2 FREE books are mine to keep.

Name _____

Street Address _____ Apt. No. _____

City _____ State _____ Zip Code _____

Telephone _____

Signature _____
(if under 18 parent or guardian must sign)

Terms and prices subject to change. Orders subject
to acceptance by True Value Home Subscription
Services, Inc.

10955

"1991 GOLDEN SPUR AWARD WINNER"

Golden Spur Awards have been given to such greats as
Nelson Nye, Louis L'Amour and Elmer Kelton. Awarded
by the Western Writers of America, it recognizes literature
and art that best portray the American West.

JOURNAL OF THE GUN YEARS

Richard Matheson

*EVERY HERO HAS HIS SECRETS.
BUT SOME LEGENDS NEVER DIE.*

Marshal Clay Halser was a legend in the Southwest. Back east
they told tall tales about Clay Halser, the Civil War Veteran who
cleaned up the West. He was a fugitive wanted for murder. An
outlaw on the run. An acquaintance of Cullen Baker and Wild
Bill Hickok. And in spite of his past, he became one of the
greatest lawmen of all time. But behind the myth—in his own
private journal—lies the true story of Marshal Clay Halser . . .

___0-425-13207-2/$4.50

For Visa, MasterCard and American Express orders ($15 minimum) call: 1-800-631-8571

**FOR MAIL ORDERS: CHECK BOOK(S). FILL
OUT COUPON. SEND TO:**

BERKLEY PUBLISHING GROUP
390 Murray Hill Pkwy., Dept. B
East Rutherford, NJ 07073

NAME_____

ADDRESS_____

CITY_____

STATE_____ZIP_____

PLEASE ALLOW 6 WEEKS FOR DELIVERY.
PRICES ARE SUBJECT TO CHANGE WITHOUT NOTICE.

POSTAGE AND HANDLING:
$1.75 for one book, 75¢ for each additional. Do not exceed $5.50.

BOOK TOTAL $ _____

POSTAGE & HANDLING $ _____

APPLICABLE SALES TAX $ _____
(CA, NJ, NY, PA)

TOTAL AMOUNT DUE $ _____

PAYABLE IN US FUNDS.
(No cash orders accepted.)

419